Life, Death and Other Distractions

Peter Rodgers

Life, Death and Other Distractions

Life, Death and Other Distractions
ISBN 978 1 76109 077 6
Copyright © Peter Rodgers 2021
Cover image: Octavo Typography

First published 2021 by
GINNINDERRA PRESS
PO Box 3461 Port Adelaide 5015
www.ginninderrapress.com.au

Contents

The spider's web of memory

The first time I was in court, I was very young and up for adoption. I remember nothing. It can't have been a success.

The second time, I wore a dark blue suit from the clothing donated to the home by the town's menswear shop.

'Very cool,' some of the other boys teased.

I didn't care about coolness. I simply wanted to look normal, unthreatening. I was much more concerned about Judge Galston's appearance than my own. He looked sickly. I worried he might be dying and determined to land a last blow for justice. A sixteen-year-old who'd done what I had could fit the bill nicely.

The judge looked at me and asked sharply, 'Was this a spur of the moment act or had you considered harming Paul Jameson for some time?'

What a dumb question I thought. How many boys carry around a can of lighter fluid and a Zippo just in case they get the urge?

All I said, though, was, 'I don't think so, sir.'

'That is of little help,' he retorted.

'If I might, Your Honour,' Rachel Summers from Legal Aid broke in, 'it may be appropriate to note that Paul had not exactly endeared himself to most of the other boys in the institution. I'm not suggesting that excuses the assault in any way, though it helps to contextualise it.'

'Thank you, Ms Summers,' said the judge, sounding irritated. Looking straight at me, he said, 'I would like you to tell me in your own words about that night.'

Which particular night, I wondered.

That winter's night when Paul Jameson grabbed the three books, the only evidence of my life before the home, and flung them on the fire, the covers bursting into bright orange-blue flames and the pages turning quickly, one by one, as if the fire itself was speed reading before everything was gone?

Or the night soon after when I poured lighter fuel over Paul's hands and flicked the Zippo into life, tempted for a moment to give his head and also his privates a good splash too?

Or the nights that followed, when the other boys pretended I'd done a terrible thing whenever the staff were around, but after lights out whispered that Paul got exactly what he deserved?

'Where'd you get the Zippo?' one boy had asked, his voice brimming with admiration.

'Found it,' I muttered.

'What's it like to set fire to someone?' he persisted.

'Try it some time,' I snapped, thinking about how I'd thrown up in the toilet afterwards. It was the smell. Not remorse.

All I said in court was, 'There's no excuse for my actions, even if those books were special. Your Honour,' I added, mimicking the refrain that flitted around the courtroom like a jingle.

I would happily have gone on to explain. How, when I had been at the home for a few years and was old enough to understand, Mrs Browning called me to her office. She held me carefully with her eyes and told me a bit about my very early life. That my father, whoever he was, had disappeared and my mother couldn't cope.

Then she picked up the books from her desk. 'These are very special,' she said. 'They were given to your mother when she was about your age.'

Call it what you will: funny, sad, silly, but I was disappointed. I'd already seen the books in the home's library, even if I hadn't read them: *The Magic Pudding*, *Black Beauty* and *Wind in the Willows*. Then I opened the covers and saw on the title pages, written in a large, careful hand, the name Susan C.

Mrs Browning let me stare at those looping blue ink trails then said quietly, 'That'll be all for now, David. Take good care of those books, won't you? They're a precious keepsake.' She put her hand on my shoulder and walked me to the door.

I ached to put my hand on top of hers and keep it there and ask her to tell me more about Susan C. All I said, though, was, 'Thank you, Mrs Browning.'

It seemed all too clear that Judge Galston would not have cared a jot about such detail. 'I am appalled by your behaviour,' he declared. 'In a carefully calculated manner, you inflicted grievous bodily harm on a sleeping boy. Many would consider that a term in an appropriate correctional institution would be entirely warranted.' He took a deep breath, reluctant it seemed to say anything more. Eventually he said, 'Nonetheless, I acknowledge certain mitigating factors.'

Paul's bullying was one of them. Another was my contrition. I had never heard of that word before Rachel Summers pumped me full of it. Contrition now leaked from me, almost like lighter fluid.

There was also another powerful factor working on me. What if Susan C heard about my court appearance? Would she be even more ashamed of her son?

In the bus on the way to court, I'd been on the verge of asking how I could track her down. 'Excuse me, Mrs Browning,' I began.

She turned to me and my nerve failed.

'Nothing really. Sorry.'

I could set another boy alight but I couldn't ask a question about my mother.

Another mitigating factor, Judge Galston said, was Mrs Browning's letter. It lay on the bench in front of him. The judge cleared his throat with a wet gurgle and read aloud a couple of passages.

To my annoyance, the first one showed sympathy for Paul. He had been 'Traumatised by events beyond his comprehension', Mrs Browning wrote. I wasn't sure what that meant but I didn't like the tone. The second passage was more helpful. Mrs Browning called me 'A young man with promise who had been unreasonably provoked'.

'Admirable,' Judge Galston declared, 'but in no way does it mediate this egregious behaviour. Let me warn you, young man, one more transgression, no matter how slight, and you will find yourself incarcerated.'

Some of the boys had warned me that judges spoke a language only other judges could understand. But I certainly got the gist.

*

That strange thing called normal life resumed: classes, sport, chores, usually under the scrutiny of the dorm master Mr Hobbs – who had a big blotched nose which always had a drip right on the end no matter what the weather was like – meals, bed, then the cycle all over again.

Paul Jameson, with his two friends Charlie Wong and Alex Hansen, seemed intent on ignoring me. I fretted about what they were planning. No longer a book-owner, I started spending time in the library, day-dreaming more than reading. Was Susan C still alive? Did she have other children? Was she happy? Sometimes I imagined that Mrs Browning was really Susan C. She had come to help me but felt awkward about revealing it, knowing it would make the other boys jealous.

If only Mrs Browning would put her hand on my shoulder again and we could talk about Susan C or books, even ourselves. I could sense the tingle on my shoulder from the touch of her hand. But the conversation, and the tingle, never came. I couldn't hold that against her. Mrs Browning had her job to do; I was part of her daily routine.

*

I worried constantly about Paul. I was used to him behaving in a particular way and could no longer rely on that. He would soon turn eighteen and leave the home. Had the prospect of life on the outside curbed his need to get even?

I was summoned to Mrs Browning's office. My imagination careered about Susan C.

Mrs Browning asked me to close the door, used both hands to carefully adjust her glasses, then fixed her keen, hazel eyes on me. 'David, I have a favour to ask of you.'

I still feel embarrassed by my reaction to this prim, caring woman who I fantasised was my mother.

'You can't be serious,' I spat.

'I'm very serious, David,' she replied calmly. 'It's important for you both to start with a clean slate.'

'What does that mean? Why are you taking his side?'

'David, I'm on both your sides. That's why I'm asking. Please.'

I sat there, choked by her betrayal.

Yet two weeks later, along with Mrs Browning and Paul, I was seated in the front room of Cathy Reid's little cottage. Paul had been helping Cathy, the home's gardener and Mrs Fixit, as she called herself, to prepare for his post-home life. We sat there, eating shortbread and sipping watery orange cordial, searching for something to look at besides each other. Paul seemed bigger, fitter and meaner looking than ever. Silently, I urged Mrs Browning and Cathy to keep chatting, to give me time to prepare, though I had thought of little else for the past weeks.

Mrs Browning kept glancing in my direction.

Finally, I took a deep breath, stood up, and said in a raspy half-whisper, 'I need to say this before you leave the home where we have lived for many years. I did a terrible thing and I am truly sorry. I hope you will forgive me and I wish you good luck.' I slumped onto the chair, perspiring even though the day was cool.

Mrs Browning nodded ever so slightly. Paul sat, a strange, indecipherable look on his face. Then he rose, walked across the room and stood in front of me, his right hand extended. At such close quarters, the pink ridges on the back of his fingers sickened me. But I had no choice. We shook hands.

Paul said brusquely, 'You and I are going outside to have a little talk.'

I looked towards Mrs Browning, desperate for rescue.

'That's fine, boys,' she said, without the slightest hint of concern.

'Come on,' Paul said.

I trailed after him, helpless in the face of such treachery, badly needing to pee. Paul led the way to a stand of untidy eucalypts, planted many years before. In their shade lay an assortment of rusting metal chairs draped in dusty layers of spider's web.

'Sit down,' he ordered.

I brushed off one of the chairs, the web sticking to my hands.

'For God's sake,' Paul said, 'just sit down and don't be such a wuss. The reason you're here is simple. You can help me.'

'I don't know what you're talking about,' I squeaked.

'Cathy says I won't get much of a job unless I can read and write better. Mrs Browning told her you could help.'

I stared at him. I couldn't believe my ears. It was a moment when crying was the most joyful human emotion.

'Well,' Paul demanded, 'yes or no, what'll we tell Mrs Browning? We don't have all day.'

'Sure,' I sniffled. I'd bitten my tongue and could taste blood in my mouth. Trying to regain control of my voice, I added, 'I'd be happy to. But I've got to take a piss before we go inside.'

He shook his head and grinned. 'Just what did you think was going to happen out here? You're such a wuss.'

*

Paul slowly lifted the carapace that hid the roiling of his early life.

'Your mum was trying to do the right thing by you,' he said one day. 'Mine never knew what hit her, my dad neither.'

'What happened?' I asked.

'Truck went through a red light and cleaned them up. Driver pissed to the eyeballs. Bastard.'

'Wasn't there anyone else to look after you?'

'Stupid bloody family rows before I was born. None of them wanted a bar of me.'

During one of our sessions, I blurted out, 'I really am sorry about your hands.'

'Must have been a weird experience for you,' Paul replied. 'Surprised you could do it. Such a goody-goody, wandering around the home with your books, reading to the other kids.' He looked at his fingers and shrugged. 'Anyway, could have been worse. You might have burned my nuts off!'

A few days before he left the home, Paul came to see me. 'I heard you really are Mrs Browning's pet now,' he said.

'What do you mean?' I asked, defensive.

'Don't be so bloody touchy! Story is that Mrs Browning wants you to become a teacher here.'

'She said I could stay on and help the other teachers while I study.'

'And?'

'I will.'

'So you bloody well should!'

*

The next time I saw Paul was at Mrs Browning's funeral, an extraordinary gathering of those linked through one diminutive figure.

Her doctor deflected clumsy attempts at interrogation about her sudden death, commenting only, 'Well, she's at peace now, that's what matters.'

Judge Galston was there, now looking truly ill and not nearly as formidable as when I first encountered him. He tapped me on the shoulder and said tersely, 'You owe that woman everything,' before shuffling away.

I felt a pulse of anger at his tone but relented. Perhaps the judge could never escape the grumpiness that being Your Honour entailed. And I could hardly disagree with him.

Paul looked even more miserable than I felt. We didn't say much. We shared the mystery of being rescued by someone who was a fixture in our lives, yet always remained an aching distance from us.

As we prepared to leave the cemetery, lit by a soulless winter sun, Paul said, 'I won't be coming to the wake, got a sick kid at home, but want you to have these.'

He handed me a small, weighty parcel wrapped in dark blue paper, Mrs Browning's favourite colour. That was one of the few personal details she had ever shared.

That night, when the home was quiet, I poured myself a drink and unwrapped the parcel. Inside were three new books. There was also a note from Paul.

Dear David,

I owe you and we both owe Mrs Browning. What we did to each other can't be undone. I'm glad we got to know each other a bit. You'll go on wondering about Susan C. When you look at these books, I hope you'll feel she's around.

The boys need someone like you here.

Good luck. Wuss!

Paul

PS: It's left to me to tell you and I had to work up to it. The driver of the truck which wiped out my parents was Mrs Browning's brother.

I sat there, staring at those familiar titles, rereading that letter, that PS, countless, countless times. I felt, at once, a pang of jealousy that such a cruel reality had been withheld from me, deep grief over the randomness of events which shattered ordinary lives, and yet relief, elation even.

Only then did I truly comprehend how memories as delicate and as powerful as a spider's web would forever bind me to the home. Once I had dreaded the thought of such institutionalisation, the very word a taunt. Now, I embraced it.

Our fern garden

The images of that terrible time are like photographs, still and studied, attempts at brave expressions and even a few watery smiles. Mum and me, Jess and Harry, Katy and Alex wearing determined, pleading faces. Inside us there was chaos and disconnection and a dense, suffocating uncertainty. We demanded an explanation that, even then, we knew we'd never get.

Gradually, we stopped asking the question. The question that had taunted us, mercilessly taunted us, when we huddled together or sat alone; taunted us in restless sleep or aching wakefulness. I don't know why we stopped. It wasn't as though the question didn't matter any more. Perhaps we just came to accept that it was pointless. Perhaps we no longer wished to embarrass him, or those he'd left behind.

Left? Surely not just that. He'd deserted. He'd crept off sometime on that warm spring afternoon with the buzz of neighbourhood Victas in our ears. I've tried so many times to imagine how he walked that day. Once, when there was no one else around, I even paced out the distance. From the front door to the garage, it took me exactly thirty-one steps. Probably took him the same, because we were very close in height. It would have taken him a good deal fewer if he had gone through the back door and scurried across the lawn, but then he would have run a bigger risk of being spotted. Anyway, I know he would have preferred using the driveway at the side of the house. It rarely got any sun and he took pride in the ferns he'd planted there. Some weekends, he'd fiddle around with them for hours. Sometimes, we kids would help him. It was cool and peaceful, with a sense of the unknown you never find in a scruffy backyard with dog turds in inconvenient places.

On that day, he must have calculated the moment very carefully so we would not hear the murmur of the car and go and check what he was doing. Was he sitting inside one moment, then he glanced at his watch and thought to himself, 'It's time, better be off'?' Did he say anything? Something really obvious, that only he knew mattered – because it would be the last time he would speak to us. Ever.

I worried for a while that he might have used the ferns as an excuse. But I like to think that he didn't, that he still had his pride.

It would have taken guts to do what he did. I know that now, though at the time all I felt was a sickened anger. I let it out perhaps more than I should have, and one day I overheard the couple down the street telling Mum that it was my way of expressing grief. Nonsense – it was rage, pure and simple.

And it wasn't just that he'd gone, it was the ordinariness of it all. Yeah, ordinariness. Lots of fathers do a bunk; but if you're going to pull that sort of stunt, put a bit of drama into it. Pick a day with some bite – maybe a big storm or a howling wind or some catastrophe that'll fix it in people's minds for years afterwards. You know the sort of thing. They'll be talking about the day the Sydney Harbour Tunnel flooded, then someone will ask, 'Wasn't that the same day as…?' and everyone will nod and say, 'Yeah, that's right and what a terrible thing that was too.'

That's how you'd do it, not hide behind the sound of lawnmowers practising for the summer.

I've thought a lot about the hours before we realised that something was wrong. They were the last truly innocent moments of my life. You'd think you'd remember the details with a mathematical exactness that would single that day out from all others. Strangely, it isn't quite like that. You remember the impact, the emotion, with a sharpness that cuts you like a razor. But some of the detail gets blurred.

What I do remember is Mum getting back from afternoon tea with Mrs Davies. It would have been about half past five, because those two could talk for hours. Mum was in a pretty good mood but that soon changed, because Jess was supposed to have started getting dinner and she hadn't done a thing. Not even peel the spuds, which I then had to do because Jess had a row with Mum. More of a mini-row really, but Jess huffed off to her room, slamming the door so hard it sounded like a car backfiring.

The others, Harry and Katy and Alex, were watching TV, which Mum didn't mind too much because it kept them more or less quiet and more or less out of her hair.

Mum and I then started working in the kitchen and she said, matter-of-factly, 'Anyone seen Dad?'

Well, the truth was we hadn't for quite a while. Which was a bit unusual when we were all at home, because it was hard not to keep bumping into one another. Still, we didn't really take much notice.

Just after the six o'clock news started, Mum asked Harry to take the garbage out. Which of course he complained about, whining that it was really Katy's turn and why did he have to do it all the time. Finally, he stirred himself and took the squashy plastic bag out to the bin at the back of the garage.

When he came in, he said, 'There's a funny smell out there.'

'What sort of a smell?' Mum asked, not very interested.

'Aw, a sort of exhausty smell,' Harry said.

'You've been sniffing your own farts again!' Katy yelped.

She and Harry are the closest in age and get on all right most of the time. But they can't help trying to score points off each other.

'That'll be enough, Katy!' Mum snapped, her post-Mrs Davies good mood now completely gone. 'Go and set the table. If you can't say something nice, say nothing.'

That was one of her favourite phrases.

'Nothing it'll be then,' Katy said defiantly. But she got up and started rooting around in the drawer for knives and forks, making as much of a racket as possible just to irritate Mum, who carefully took no notice.

I do remember when we found him – six forty-eight p.m. I didn't know that then because when Jess yelled out from upstairs that there was smoke coming from the garage, the last thing I did was look at my watch and make a mental note of the time. But afterwards, when the police and the ambulance arrived, they asked when we discovered the body and Harry said around seven and at the inquest I heard that time read out.

It wasn't really smoke – at least not the sort that happens when your garage burns down. The streetlight in front of our house must have given the fumes the appearance of ordinary smoke. But there's nothing ordinary about the stuff that's just killed your dad.

We rushed out to the garage, Mum yelling, 'Get the car keys, find the car keys somebody, quickly, get the car out, get the car out before it burns!'

I'm not sure how much we took that in but, in our panic, I do remember a couple of things pretty clearly – the darkness and silence of the garage, and how tightly the door was closed. I don't know who first caught on that there was no fire but something much, much worse. I have a feeling it might have been Mum or me but, afterwards, when we talked about it, I think it was pretty much all of us at the same time, except Alex, who was a bit young.

Even before we got the door open properly, my mother cried out. I wish I could describe that sound adequately but I can't except that it seemed to come from deep inside her and build up such enormous pressure that when it finally burst out it left her gasping on the driveway. I fumbled for the light and a wave of horror washed over us as we took in the detail of what had happened and what would be forever. We started wailing and I beat my fists against the car and cursed my father viciously.

By the time the ambulance arrived, most of our neighbours were there. They had carried my mother inside and laid her on a bed and placed blankets around our shoulders as though we were survivors from some horrific accident. Someone made my mother a cup of tea, which she promptly vomited, along with Mrs Davies's chocolate cake, on the bedroom floor. I'm sure it was my mother's distress, not her pool of sick, that made me throw up too. I rushed into the bathroom and found Katy and Jess and Harry all kneeling and retching into the bath, tears streaming down their faces.

'How could he do this to us, how could he do this to us?' we cried and cried and cried, like a terrible, ancient chant.

When finally I came out, Alex was sitting rigid in front of the TV. I held him for a long, long while, feeling his shock and grief gradually melt into me.

*

The coroner, Mr Harris, was a small, frail-looking man dressed in grey like a caricature, but with dark, quick eyes and a busy mouth that seemed at constant risk of not closing properly. We had left Alex with Mrs Davies but the rest of us sat before the coroner, neatly dressed as if being auditioned for our part in this tragic incident as he called it. Mr Harris gave my mother a look of stern, official sympathy and asked if she had any inkling of what was in Dad's mind.

She answered, 'No, none at all,' so softly he asked her to repeat it.

What an insult of a question, I thought. How can you possibly answer it in any dignified way? The person you've lived with for sixteen years is about to kill himself and you have no idea. That must make you look really dumb or insensitive or suggest that it was a completely hopeless relationship. Which it wasn't, not by a long shot.

But what if you say, 'Yes'? Does that make you an accomplice? Are you meant to have pleaded, cajoled, perhaps even threatened? But what sort of threat can you make to a husband who wants to kill himself? Isn't he in quarantine? If you do threaten, don't you give him an extra reason for the act?

And what did this little grey man with the ill-fitting lips mean by inkling? At first, I thought the word had come off the top of his head. Maybe in yesterday's hearings he'd used idea or notion or hint so today he was going for a bit of variety. But it was no accident. I saw just how deliberate and how clever that word was. I saw it on his face as my poor mother half-whispered her answer. I saw it in his disbelieving look that said, 'You mean you were together all those years, and yet…'

I wanted to yell out, 'Stop it, you bastard, stop it! My father's killed himself and now you blame my mother. How can you do this to her, on top of everything else? How can you?' The words ran round and round inside my head and twice I took a deep breath, preparing to shout the reply that would ring in everybody's ears. But in the end I kept quiet and squeezed my mother's hand so tight I heard her knuckles crack. She gave me a sad half-smile and I could see the tears in her eyes.

Mr Harris stopped talking and a policeman began in the flat voice that all police seem to use even when they're reporting truly awful events like a dad who has suicided. When he talked about the garage and how well built it was with few gaps or cracks and that there seemed no possibility it was an accident, I wondered, out of nowhere, if Dad would still be alive if we'd put up a carport. Then he would have had to risk doing it in full view, with a hose stuck in the car window, or have driven away – and he could hardly have done that without making a better fist of saying goodbye than he did.

*

On our way home from the coroner, we stopped at a café. Mum had a cup of tea and we kids had a soft drink. Mum ordered a couple of plates of mixed sandwiches for us to share. Though she didn't say anything, I think she was a bit surprised we didn't start squabbling over who got to eat what. But it was hard to muster the energy to say anything, let alone have a fight. So we sat there listening to each other chewing. Whenever I hear someone chewing loudly, I think of that day.

I thought about Dad's cremation. I hadn't even known what a wake was until they were making the arrangements for the service and Mrs Davies said to Mum, 'You've got enough on your mind. Leave the wake to me.'

Later, Mum told me that a wake was a bit like a party to celebrate the life of the person who died. But, as she said that, she bit her lip and a bright red dot of blood appeared.

Sitting in the café, I thought about the wake, and about Mr Harris, and about what a cruel thing language can be.

*

Two weeks after the funeral, we kids were sitting in the lounge room when the phone rang.

Katy answered it and a puzzled look crept over her face. 'It's that real estate agent from the next suburb,' she said. 'He wants to speak to the man of the house.' She said these last words mockingly, with the mouthpiece only half-covered. Then she asked us quietly, 'Do we have one now? Is it Mum?' Her eyes glistened.

I took the phone from her and said, 'Hello.' I remember feeling embarrassed that my voice sounded high and uncertain.

'Good morning, young man,' the voice said. 'To whom do I have the pleasure of speaking?'

I mouthed these words to the other kids. They didn't get them all. But they could see I was sending the agent up, so they started making faces and laughing. Even Katy seemed to cheer up.

'It's Derek.'

'Well, Derek, let me begin by offering our very sincere condolences on the tragic loss of your father. Such a shock. These cannot be easy times for you, we know. And your poor mother. Poor woman, to think that after all these years…' His voice trailed off as if to emphasise the bond of grief between us but I could sense his fingers tapping impatiently on the desk.

'What's this about?' I asked.

'We simply wanted you to know that if at any time, any time at all, your mother feels she needs to make a fresh start for the family, somewhere without the – how shall I put it – without the memories of your current dwelling, we stand ready to assist in any way possible.'

'You're saying we should move?'

'Not at all, not at all. That's a matter entirely for your own decision. I simply wanted you to know that if the time comes when you feel burdened by,' he paused, 'by recent events, we can assure you of the utmost discretion in handling the practical requirements of the situation.'

'What do you mean? That you won't tell the buyer that Dad killed himself in the garage and the place is haunted?'

That set him back a bit, I could tell by the silence. But he recovered and said, patronisingly, 'Of course, you'll want to discuss the whole matter with your mother. Please tell her that if there's anything we can do, anything at all, we're as close as the nearest phone.'

I said nothing and hung up.

*

We never said a word to Mum about the phone call. Maybe that poncy-sounding agent, or possibly some other, spoke directly to her but she didn't say anything to us. That one call made us more determined than ever to stay put, partly for Mum's sake, partly for our own and, funnily enough, partly for Dad's. The memories of him around the place were not all bad.

He'd been pretty good with his hands, for example, and put in a new staircase which is still there, as sturdy as the day he finished it. Even now I can sense my father's touch in the wood, which he had lovingly shaped and polished till it glistened in the morning light like the finest glass.

Dad did let us down badly, and occasionally I still feel sharp pulses of anger towards him. For a while I would never say, 'My father's dead' or 'My father died.' I wasn't going to let him off that lightly, so it was always, 'My father killed himself.'

Gradually, I stopped insisting on that phrase, just the same way we stopped asking that question. I don't know why he did what he did. I don't think it was a lack of love for us. Maybe it was a lack of love for himself, the sort you need to go on living.

One thing we have done is to take down the garage and replace it with a carport. We must be the only ones around here ever to have done that. And the strange thing is since then the ferns have never looked

22

better. It must have changed the light or the breezes, something like that. I know that probably sounds weird and the people down the road keep telling us that ferns don't like too much of either. So it's something of a mystery. Mum says we have to accept that there are things we'll never know whether it's about plants or people. What really matters now is that the ferns look great. We're very proud of them. No visitor ever leaves without a tour of our fern garden.

The right call?

I'd prepared very carefully for the talk with my dog, Asteroid, knowing it would be a turning point in our relationship. If I'd seen where it would lead, I would have kept my mouth shut.

The talk was about life's hardest truth – that time runs out for us all. In Asteroid's case, I'd decided it was more a question of money. I simply couldn't afford his vet bills any more.

'I have some good news and I have some bad news,' I told him. 'The good news is that I'm more than happy to go on feeding and housing you to the current high standard. There aren't many other dogs,' I added a bit smugly, 'who eat kangaroo fillet every second night. The bad news is that I've capped your future veterinary expenses at $1,750. Once that's gone, so are you. In fact, the last $75 is earmarked for your final injection.'

Asteroid gave me one of his you-must-feel-guilty-to-your-core looks.

I broke the awkward silence saying, 'Of course, you can build up credit.'

'Just how can I do that?' he grumped. 'After all, I'm only a dog.'

'Well, for a start, the rabbits are a problem in the garden. So for each one you catch and show me, there'll be a bonus of $30.'

'Why don't I just eat it?'

'Well, of course, and that would certainly save on kangaroo fillet, but I'll have to register it first.'

'Register it?'

'I bought this pocket ledger when I was at the newsagent earlier in the week.' I fished the smart red book out of my pocket and opened it to the first page. 'See, there's $1,750 in your credit column already and nothing on the debit side. I think a $30 bonus per rabbit is entirely reasonable.'

'You've really worked it all out, haven't you?' Asteroid said, his tone acidic. 'And you know I have a problem with arthritis.'

'I do, and that's why I'm more than happy to spend up on your krill oil tablets. But a bit more exercise would do you the world of good.'

Asteroid thought for a moment then said, 'Make it $40 a rabbit and I'll give it a go.'

'$35 tops. It's all I can afford.'

'Let's do it this way: $35 for the first six months, then $40.'

'You drive a hard bargain,' I said.

'Well, it's my life we're talking about here,' Asteroid replied. 'And if we're working out bonuses, we're not going to stop at rabbits. What about all those visits to your mother? You know it gives her a lot of pleasure seeing me. That must count for something.'

'Fair point,' I agreed. 'For each future visit, I'll add another $20.'

'Only $20! Are you really saying that a dead rabbit is worth more than your live mother?'

'Of course not! But are you saying it's harder work visiting my mother than it is catching a rabbit? Don't push your luck.'

'Okay,' Asteroid conceded, 'but there are two other things. The first is that I can talk, the second is that I don't chase cats. Both of those have got to be worth serious dollars.'

'But all dogs, at least the ones I've had anything to do with, can communicate with their masters. It's –'

'Communicate! What do you mean communicate?' Asteroid demanded. 'You and I talk. There's a world of difference and you know it. Think of all the conversations we've had over the years on everything from growing lettuces to Sophoclean tragedies to Sinus-American rivalry. When your wife ran away with the travel agent you told me it was only our heart-to-heart chats that got you through. I suppose you've forgotten all that?'

'No, I haven't, and you have been a very special friend with very special talents and it's only right you mention them. I'll think about a bonus. By the way, it's *Sino*-American rivalry.'

'Is that so? Well, by the way,' he mimicked, 'please explain that non-sense about dogs and their masters. I've always regarded you as an equal.'

'Just a figure of speech,' I replied. 'Don't take it to heart.'

'Cats?' Asteroid persisted.

'What about them?' I asked. 'Some dogs dislike them, others don't. You just happen to be in the second category.'

'Sometimes you truly astound me,' Asteroid said, shaking his head. 'I happen to be in the so-called second category only because of what you did to me as a pup. Yeah, I know you don't like to talk about it and I really do appreciate you calling me "him" in front of our friends. But rarely a day goes by when I don't wonder what it would be like to scare the living daylights out of a cat. I see one and my breathing gets shallow and my pulse races. A bit like you when you bring one of your girl-friends home and you're walking behind her to the house. I can practi-cally see what you're thinking.'

'Excuse me!' I interrupted.

'I'm not trying to make you feel guilty, just the point that I may not act on my impulses the way other dogs do but I still feel something, operation or no operation. I have to exercise self-control the way an al-coholic does.'

'I hardly think it's on a par with AA,' I said, 'but I'll give it some thought.'

We sat in silence on the porch, looking out over the valley and the little puddles of smoke from early autumn fires.

Asteroid gave me one of his serious looks and said, 'You do think that dogs are men's and women's best friend, don't you?'

'Of course,' I said, 'without a doubt.'

'Don't you think it a bit odd that you've just put me on quota but you won't do the same for your mother?'

'What on earth does she have to do with this?'

'Look at me. Overall, I'm in pretty reasonable shape, still enjoying life. Look at your mum. Wonderful lady, I know, but there's only one way she'll leave the nursing home. Yet you go on pouring money into looking after her, strikes me as all a bit sad, not just for her but for you.'

'Now look here –' I began but Asteroid cut me off.

'I know this is hard to hear, but if the ledger system is good enough for me, your best friend, it should be good enough for others, especially those you love most.'

'Just what are you getting at?' I asked.

'That we devise a rating system for humans and animals over a certain age,' he replied calmly. 'It would measure their quality of life and their prospects and put a limit on how much would be spent on them.'

'Sounds suspiciously like euthanasia. And by animals I presume you mean dogs?'

'Well, it's not really euthanasia, just that everyone would know exactly how much they have to play with, so to speak, and of course they'd be able to top it up by making themselves useful. You've provided the model in what you're doing with me. I'm simply suggesting we apply it more broadly. And yes, I do mean dogs, at least for a start. After all we're the ones closest to humans.'

'I thought monkeys had that honour, if that's the right word.'

'C'mon,' Asteroid despaired, 'monkeys might claim that but no one in their right mind believes them. Just how many people keep monkeys as pets? When did you last see a sniffer monkey, let alone a guide one? Monkeys are out for themselves. Actually, I suppose that does make them very much like people. So okay then,' he shrugged, 'if you'd rather work with a monkey, fine by me, just give me the $1,750 and I'll get out of your hair.'

'All right, all right,' I said, 'calm down. Of course, I see us as a team. I just feel a bit nervous about what we're taking on.'

Our rating system prompted parliamentary and pub debate across the nation and a social media storm. Many lauded our imagination and courage. We were given a fifteen-minute slot each week on ABC television called *Earning Your Keep*. It drew record audiences. Asteroid received approaches from major publishers for a practical guide on teaching dogs to talk. He declined, saying they either had it them or they didn't. I thought that was a bit brusque. Asteroid insisted we concentrate on the job at hand.

We had our critics, especially in the media and the churches. 'Keep your paws off our grannies!' screamed some the headlines. Prominent religious figures came out of sometimes forced retirement to lead a campaign against what they labelled 'This evil book of death'. Our friends fretted about our well-being, but we laughed off their concerns. The vitriol was no worse than we'd expected. We persisted.

Then that fateful Saturday when we travelled to Sydney to participate in a public debate at no less a venue than the Town Hall. It was a calm, sparkling evening. We arrived as the sun was setting behind the magnificent old building. It was great to be alive, to be pursuing a just and timely cause. We stood on the kerb opposite the Town Hall waiting for the lights to change. Suddenly, out of the crowd on the other side there appeared a large, orange tabby cat. It gave us a mean, challenging look.

Without warning, inexplicably, Asteroid took off, barrelling across the road. I yelled to him. He had eyes only for the cat. Asteroid was smart, incredibly smart. But he was no longer agile. He was also a country dog, unused to city traffic.

'These things do happen,' said the vet at the twenty-four-hour practice in the Haymarket, to where I rushed Asteroid in the back of a taxi after agreeing to pay triple fare to compensate for any bloodstains. I cradled Asteroid all the way. He was comatose, I was in shock.

The vet's tone was flat, nasal and completely uninterested. The closest he got to sympathy was another throwaway remark: 'If it makes you feel any better, he wouldn't have suffered much.'

That did not help one jot. In the awful days afterwards, the only thing that salved my despair was the way Asteroid's many admirers rallied to keep his memory alive. Their efforts warmed and saddened me at the same time.

Three months after his death, with the blessing of the Sydney City Council, we unveiled a small bronze plaque on the pavement opposite the Town Hall. It was nothing pretentious. But his lovingly sculpted image and the simple tribute, 'Asteroid – a true pioneer', reminded all who saw it of what we'd lost. A group of us shared the cost of the plaque. That worked out at exactly $75 each, the sum I'd allocated for Asteroid's farewell injection.

The irony of that figure still haunts me. Much worse is the fact that I've walked away from the cause for which Asteroid died. I could point to the fact that the police urged me to adopt a low profile, as they put it, and my friends tell me I'm just being prudent. The terrible truth though is that, at heart, I'm a coward.

The day after the memorial ceremony, I received a voicemail from someone claiming to represent 'The Friends of Life'. The message said, 'We got the dog, we'll get you if we have to, and we won't use a cat. Your call.'

I had no choice really.

Did I?

Colonel and Mrs Smith's special day out

Colonel Smith

I can't tell you how my heart sank as I watched her drive off that first afternoon. I knew it was for the best, of course. Just not right her having to lug me around at home, doing things a wife shouldn't have to. The modifications to the house helped. But it was all such a strain, I could see that.

I'd never imagined my old age being quite so rickety, my life ticking down like this. Once you're in here, this home-away-from-home as it styles itself, it really hits you. A one-way ticket, that's what we have now. I try to joke about it with the others. Better make friends quickly, I tell the newcomers. Never know who'll be checking out next. Some of them get it. Others, well, it's plain as day they're a lost cause.

Mrs Smith

When he first moved, I felt such despair, his and mine. It stirred me in the cold, black hours, alone in the bed we'd shared for all those years. Who would have thought I'd miss his fastidiousness the way I have? Poor man, finding himself among all those strangers with their different ways.

It's what you're accustomed to dear, I soothed.

Mrs Smith, he replied, it's what you allow yourself to become accustomed to. We must always set the bar high. That's long been one of his favourite phrases. He'll be remembered for that term alone, one of his army friends joked with me one day.

Occasionally, I wonder what I'll be remembered for. I do hope there's some small tic which will fix me fondly in other's minds after I'm gone. Silly to worry about such things, but I do.

Andrew's helped as best he could, but I can't expect him to be running over here all the time. He's so busy with his university work. Seems happy enough, all things considered.

Mrs Maxwell

The Smiths are the lucky ones, truly lucky, mark my words. So companionable. You don't see that much at their age. Mostly of course it's because one of them is dead. Even when that's not the case, even if they're both in here, often they seem little more than shadows in each other's lives.

Not with the Smiths! Regular as anything she collects him and off they tootle in that little car of theirs. Mind you, he has a lot of trouble getting into it these days. And I hear she's quite absent-minded on the road. I'm surprised really she still has a licence. I guess that's one advantage of being old, there's less to lose if you're accidentally killed. When he first came here, they actually went to concerts in the city, classical music, not my thing really. These days, seems it's just a drive, maybe afternoon tea with friends.

Andrew Smith

What a milestone, hard to believe he's made it. Especially after what happened to Margaret. Talk about it as a family, many of my friends urged. But we never were ones to open our veins like that. We ground our way through it, that's how we coped.

Mrs Smith

We've stopped going to concerts now. It was quite a task manoeuvring him about, but that's not the reason. After our last concert – the usual line-up, Mozart, Sibelius, Beethoven – we were on our way home and he said to me, I don't think I can bear all that beauty any more, it makes me feel so pointless.

That's quite possibly the saddest thing anyone's ever said to me. I don't think he's right, either. Beauty should fill us with wonder, not gloom. I've never been one to argue with him, though.

Mrs Maxwell

Popped into his room a few minutes ago. Would you believe it, there he was sporting a coat and tie! Must have taken him hours to get dressed, being the way he is. He could have asked for help. It's always ready to hand here, not like so many other places. I make sure of that. But that's not his way.

Well, well, well, I teased, dressed to the nines, eh, Colonel? He likes being called that. Quick as anything, he said, You mean the nineties, Mrs Maxwell! We both had a good chuckle.

Got something planned then? I asked. I knew it was his birthday, of course. I know most things that go on around here.

Mrs Smith and I have something quite special in mind, he said, smiling to himself. He's called her Mrs Smith for as long as I'm aware, never Bronnie or B like her friends do. I like that old-fashioned quality about him. Must come from his army days. Mind you, she definitely is Mrs Smith, a woman who knows what she's about. Bit like myself really.

Colonel Smith

Ticked myself off this morning, I did. Calm down, Colonel, I warned. It takes time to get things done, don't be so hard on yourself.

Ninety today! Even the staff seem impressed. Occasionally, I find myself wondering what it would be like to be one of them. To be twenty-five, maybe thirty, again. That age of invincibility, of wide-open dreams. When I think hard on it, I can almost bring back that feeling. Almost.

She'll be here soon. She's been a miracle. We've been a miracle. Always known what's what, never been ditherers. Like when we both gave up smoking. Went cold turkey. I wasn't sure I could do it. Lift the bar high, she teased. And we did.

There's hardly been a cross word between us. Ever. A bit of uncertainty now about whether we should say anything to Andrew. Only to be expected, I suppose. I'm pretty sure she's come around to my way of thinking.

Andrew Smith

Just your father and me for lunch on the big day, Mum said, when I phoned her last week. I hope you don't mind, she added.

Frankly, it was a relief.

No doubt it's a common story with elderly parents. They don't always appreciate the time pressures on others. Still, I have to give them credit. They read quite a bit of what I write. Occasionally, they ask a surprisingly pertinent question for people who've never been to India.

I know they'll make it a special occasion. They've always been good like that.

Mrs Smith

Penny for your thoughts? I asked him one night, restarting the conversation.

Thinking about Andrew, he replied.

He's a good boy, I said, he's done us proud. I just wish he'd find someone special. Particularly after what happened to Margaret. They were so close. Tragic.

Tragic for us all, he said, a meteor which shattered our little world.

I hope he'll be all right when we're not here, I said.

Colonel Smith

I could feel her longing to be comforted, about what's happened and what will happen. I didn't want to let her down, I ached to find the right words. But they just wouldn't come. It's always been a bit tricky that way.

My mind went to the time Andrew did that research trip to India and wrote about that sati business. It all seemed pretty gruesome to me, widows burning themselves, everyone looking on, cheering. I read that some woman did herself in that way only a couple of years back, even though they're not supposed to any more. Local officials put it down to suicide because no one made her do it. Pretty fine distinction if you ask me.

Mrs Smith

What would you do, Mrs S? he asked me one night. We'd been sitting out on the patio, talking about Andrew's article.

I'd be on your pyre in an instant, I replied.

A good idea too, he said.

We had a bit of a laugh.

There was a long pause, then he added, I wouldn't want to be here without you.

Likewise, I said.

Colonel Smith

There's no need to make a fuss. Let others think what they will. The important thing is to plan ahead, pay attention to the logistics, a lesson from my early army days.

Mrs Smith

I've always loved the view from here. The blue water dazzling in the sunlight, the wind rustling through trees much, much older than we are.

Hearing that sound now takes me back to the day a thought just popped into my head and I said to him, some trees are strange, aren't they?

What do you mean? he asked.

Well, they're naked in winter then overdress in summer and spend their days drooping from the heat.

He shook his head, laughed and said, you have a remarkable way of seeing this topsy-turvy world, Mrs Smith. Then he just sat there, smiling at me.

At that moment, I felt content more than I ever thought possible.

I so wish I could bring back that feeling now. And that we could talk to others. It might make for awkward goodbyes, but wouldn't that be wiser?

Still, a pact is a pact. It's hard to believe the day is here.

Mrs Smith/Colonel Smith

(They hold hands and kiss lightly.)

It's time.

Mrs Maxwell

Some birthday celebration all right. Where can they possibly be? They're always back precisely when they said they would. You can set your watch by it! I'd better phone the son, just to be on the safe side.

Coroner

The known facts are that these: Mrs Bronwyn Smith arrived at the Tranquil Bay Nursing Home at approximately twelve twenty-five p.m. on the day of the incident. There, she collected her husband, Colonel, Retired, Phillip Smith DSM, and they proceeded to the Pisces restaurant for lunch. Mrs Smith had made a booking earlier that week. I note it was Colonel Smith's birthday and it was customary for the couple to celebrate this event. I note also that close friends of the couple, who usually joined them on such an occasion, were not invited. Colonel and Mrs Smith departed the restaurant at two twenty p.m. They appeared to be in good spirits. At four fifty p.m., the Tranquil Bay Nursing Home director, Mrs Joanne Maxwell, phoned their son, Professor Andrew Smith, to inform him that his parents had not returned at the time they had designated, namely four p.m. She described this behaviour as out of character. At five fifteen p.m., Professor Smith arrived at his parents' residence. He located them in the living room, slumped unconscious on the lounge. Professor Smith immediately called triple zero and the ambulance and police attended promptly. Colonel and Mrs Smith were pronounced dead at the scene. Subsequent tests determined that they had consumed significant quantities of prescription painkillers as well as alcohol. An empty bottle of French champagne and two champagne glasses were retrieved from the living room. I note that the room appears to have been decorated with roses, a flower for which the Smiths had won many awards. Colonel and Mrs Smith left nothing written which might offer an insight into their mental state. According to Professor Smith's testimony, they had been deeply shocked by the accidental drowning death of their daughter and Professor Smith's twin sister, Margaret, three years earlier. Colonel Smith had suffered severe physical decline in recent years. On the evidence available to me, I can only conclude that Colonel Phillip Smith and Mrs Bronwyn Smith died from actions they had taken to ensure their decease.

Andrew Smith

Our Dearest Andrew

We were old, and our time was not far off.

Why now, you might ask? To which we could only respond, why not now?

To understand the limit of your life is a great liberation.

Forgive us and rejoice. We are with Margaret again.

Your loving Mother and Father

(Sitting in his father's study, Andrew writes this letter. These are the very words they would have used he tells himself, over and over again. Does this reassure him? Hardly. For beneath his grief and shock another feeling lurks, sharp and resolute. A bitter taste of betrayal. It comes with not being trusted.)

Comeuppance

'How dare you?!' she cried when she first heard those words. The arrogance of that man. He did not speak for her. No way.

Yet, when she thought about it, he had done her a great favour. He'd lit a fuse within. Her life's task was now clear. She wrote out a list of what she'd need: a good map, publicity, most of all a reliable rocket. They were so readily available these days on eBay or Amazon or Gumtree. But she'd need something special. The thought of the cost made her shudder. She'd have to stand out from all the other go-fund-me hopefuls.

Maybe the Queen would help. Could be just the project to take the royal mind off family troubles. Elon Musk might chip in. After all, what she had in mind was highly innovative. Vlad Putin might also lend a hand. He was a big supporter of the underdog and seemed to share her love of horses.

She wondered about a round robin email but decided a one-on-one approach was best. She'd long been complimented on her handwriting, a personal letter to the Queen might do the trick.

She hoped her sponsors, whoever they turned out to be, wouldn't get ideas about coming with her. She'd always hated brushing her teeth in front of others. Besides, she'd need downtime to polish her speech.

Her words and deeds would shake the universe.

'One small step for man, one giant leap for mankind! Just who'd you think you were fooling, Neil Armstrong, ignoring half the people on the planet?'

'My journey is for them, my one small step for them.'

At this point, she would thrust out her arms and cry, 'And look, no namby-pamby gear for me. I want intimate, authentic contact with the moon. That's why I'm going barefoot.'

Win-win

I thought it was a great line. So did my mother when I tried it on her.

A multilayered strategy, she called it. 'Publishers reject your book. You go ahead with your plan, which of course you'll have to, and the book becomes a best-seller no matter how terrible it is.' She paused, then added, 'I will miss you, though.'

I was relieved to hear that. Her enthusiastic tone had a down side. Next day, queueing in front of the visiting publisher, I took a deep breath and not bothering with preliminaries announced, 'If you won't publish my book, I'll shoot myself.'

She stared at me over horn-rimmed glasses. 'Do you know that's the third time I've heard that pitch just today?' She glanced at her watch. 'And it's only eleven a.m. If only someone would mean it,' she sighed.

'I do,' I pleaded.

'Have you told your wife?'

'Don't have one, but I've told my mother.'

'That's encouraging. Do you have a gun?'

'Not a problem. My uncle belongs to a pistol club.'

She thought for a moment. 'Tell you what. I could lend you mine. If you're serious, this could work wonders for us both.'

'I don't suppose I could have an advance?' I asked.

'You must be joking!' she snapped. 'Yours is the final, desperate act of the perennially spurned writer. One that'll possibly make you a household name. Now you want payment up front. Don't you realise how that would damage both our reputations.'

'Mmm, fair point,' I conceded. 'I'm just a bit overwhelmed at the thought of finally being in print. Don't you want some idea of what the book's about?'

'It's about you,' she exclaimed, 'your pain, your despair, your ultimate sacrifice. Always a winning formula. Just leave the details to me.'

She glanced over my shoulder and said, 'My goodness, just look at that queue. You'll have to go, so here's the deal. I promise not to publish your book, at least for now. You know what you have to do in return.'

'Done,' I said, holding out my hand, 'I'll die a happy man.'

'Some days,' she smiled, 'it's such a joy being a publisher, helping others touch their dreams.' She paused and said sternly, 'Just make sure I get my gun back.'

'Relax,' I said. 'My mother will sort it.'

Why the Phyllites were never a household name

It was so different at first. Barry could do that. Inspire us – well, at least Merv and me.

'You're a fucking genius,' Barry exclaimed when I first gave him the idea.

It was a beautiful day, brilliant blue sky, crisp, invigorating air. If my mother had been there, she'd have called it a Goldilocks day. But I could never really picture her in a prison exercise yard.

'What's it mean?' asked Merv.

'Simple,' I said. 'Barry wants to destroy Western Civilisation. It's the perfect weapon.'

'Hang on,' Barry said. 'I don't want to destroy Western Civilisation. There are some good things about it. Like flushing toilets and holiday pay. I just want to punish it, reform it. For what it did to my parents.'

''Cause they killed themselves on the grog?' Merv queried.

'Spot on. I want to obliterate alcohol, starting with wine. That's where Jake's idea comes in. How do you spell it again?' he asked, turning to me.

I spelt the word. Phylloxera.

'And you're sure it can work?'

'Well, Fi studied chemistry in high school. She got interested in wine when she worked at Dan Murphy's. Learnt quite a bit about vine diseases and that sort of stuff. She's a smart lady, should be able to come up with a new strain of phylloxera that'll ruin vineyards everywhere.'

'When does she get out?'

'Must be about the same time as you. Lucky she got caught when she did. If she'd embezzled any more, she'd have copped a really long stretch. I'll be out a bit later. Can't wait to see her!'

'Timing couldn't be better,' said Barry. 'She can brew up a few batches while we're waiting for you. Then we'll spread it around the globe.'

'Can I do the FFF…French vineyards?' asked Merv. 'I've never been to Paris.'

'Course you can, mate,' Barry replied.

He was like that. Genuinely cared for the underdog and had the size and the smarts to back it up. Right from the start, he'd taken Merv under his wing. With his red hair and freckles, his dumpy little body, that name, Mervyn, and most of all his problem with the sound eff, Merv was an obvious target for any inmate with a nasty streak. Which was most of them. Just imagine what it's like being in gaol and unable to say 'fuck' with any menace.

'I've been thinking,' I said to Barry not long after I'd given him the word. 'Maybe we should call ourselves something.'

'What do you mean?' Barry asked.

'We want to change the way people live. We should have a name. It'd be a handy recruiting tool. Remember, we'll need to cover a lot of vineyards.'

'What about the fff…fff,' Merv sounded like he was blowing up a balloon.

'Spit it out, mate,' Barry encouraged.

'Fff…Phylloxerites,' Merv said, with a minor explosion.

'Too obvious,' I said.

Merv thought for a bit. 'Got it,' he said, excited. 'The fff…Phyllites. We could start a new religion and get a tax break.'

'What on earth are you going on about?' Barry scowled.

'Well, I told you already,' Merv said. 'I was in the tax office. Before…' His lip quivered and I thought he was about to cry. He shuddered on, 'Before I came here. In one job, I processed applications from groups wanting to dodge tax because they were religious.'

'What happened?' I asked.

'They had to fff…fill out this fff…form –'

'No, I don't mean that,' I said, more sharply than I'd intended. 'How'd you end up in here?'

Merv looked at Barry.

'Go on, you better tell him,' said Barry.

'I got a new shed,' said Merv.

I stared at him. 'Eh?'

'I ran out of space for my model trains. So this bloke built a new shed for me.'

'What'd he get in return?'

'Well, he was about to be done over by the tax office. My tip-off gave him time to bury a few bodies. It's a great shed, by the way, holds all my trains. They couldn't prove it was stolen, so I got to keep it.'

'You two have quite a bit in common,' said Barry. 'Geniuses one minute, fuckwits the next.' He looked at me. 'Okay, Jake, your turn. It'll make Merv feel better about himself.'

'Do I have to?' I whined.

'We're a team. Everything out in the open!'

'Well, um,' I played for time, 'I was working on a vineyard near Orange –'

'So that's how you know about that fff…phylloxa stuff,' Merv exclaimed.

'I liberated a couple of expensive candlesticks from the owner's house. Made the mistake of offloading them at the very antique shop where he'd bought them.'

'Useless dick,' Barry laughed. 'Now, both of you, any other awkward stuff to confess while we're at it?'

Merv and I shook our heads.

*

We weren't supposed to have secrets from each other. That's why what happened later was so hurtful. But one thing I was determined that no one, most of all Barry, should hear about was my parents' first visit.

Mum came all prepared. She'd obviously read the *Family Handbook for First Timers* produced by the Corrections Service. 'Did you know,' she said brightly, 'if you were in Mannus gaol rather than Bathurst, I could bring you fresh lettuce and carrots. You always loved carrots, even when you were little and found them hard to chew.'

'Mum,' I despaired, 'Manus is in Papua New Guinea and there's no way I'm going there.'

'That's an entirely different Mannus,' she said, sniffing at my ignorance. 'This one has two ens and is near Tumbarumba. You have heard of that, haven't you? If you were there, we could bring you one loaf of bread, or,' she emphasised that word, 'one packet of bread rolls, or, one packet of flat bread. Which would you prefer?'

'Mum,' I pleaded. If anyone overheard this conversation, I'd be the laughing stock of the gaol. She sailed on. 'We could bring a meat tray to Mannus, as long as there's no marinated meat, which seems a bit silly if you ask me, but then I suppose some people might marinate the chops, which are allowed, in red wine, which isn't, and we could have a nice barbecue, the equipment for which is supplied free of charge, and would you prefer tomato or barbecue sauce, because it's one or the other, not both, and we'll have to use plastic cutlery but that'll make it more of a picnic anyway and maybe you'd like to invite a friend or two. You do have some friends, I hope, I do so miss seeing Fi, poor girl just made a silly mistake.'

'Mum, please, please,' I said, barely above a whisper, 'I promise I'll talk to the warder.'

'Is there something wrong with your throat, son?' Dad asked.

'Next time, I'll bring you some lozenges,' my mother chimed. 'They better be allowed or I'll talk to the warder.'

*

'I suppose we'll need some guiding principles for our new religion,' I said at breakfast one day.

'If we want a tax break, then definitely,' Merv replied, 'and we'll also need a Supreme Being.'

'What's that?' Barry asked.

'Something that explains how we got here.'

'Fucking criminal court, that's how,' Barry said, adding quickly, 'just joking. How do we explain what this Supreme thingamabob does?'

'I don't think we need to,' I said, 'as long as it sounds mysterious and profound.'

'You're on the right track, Jakey,' Merv smiled.

'What have we got so far?' Barry asked.

'Principle number one,' I said, 'a Supreme Being. Principle number two?'

'Getting rid of the grog,' said Barry.

'People might mistake us for Muslims,' Merv said, looking worried.

'What about calling principle two the Mission,' I suggested.

'I like that,' Barry said.

'We'll need a third principle to get the tax break,' said Merv.

'Might be a bit hard,' said Barry.

'A riddle,' I said.

'That's it, that's it,' Merv cried. 'The Riddle. Now just one other thing. What are our KPIs?'

'KP whats?' Barry demanded.

'You haven't heard of Key Performance Indicators? The tax office was fff...full of them. How do we measure the success of what we're trying to do?'

'Can you do that with a religion?' I asked.

'There'll be less cirrhosis,' Barry offered

'Hard to prove,' I said.

'You don't have to prove anything,' Merv declared. 'That's the whole point of religion. People fff...fff...feel better because they believe they will. Our job is simple: download and fff...fill out the fff...form. We can't lose.'

'One thing still bothers me,' said Barry. 'We're about to start a new religion to rescue Western Civilisation. Yet its three founding members are all in gaol. That's not a promising start.'

'Nothing to fff…fret about,' Merv said, shaking his head. 'We saw the fff…folly of our ways. That sort of line always goes over well.'

We were on a high. We were on a search for truth. And we found a hard one very quickly. Prison is a not a congenial environment in which to launch a rescue mission for any civilisation.

'We'll need a critical mass of adherents,' said Merv, 'otherwise our application for tax-free status will definitely get the thumbs down.'

Three people turned up at each of the two meetings we were given permission to organise.

'I thought a couple of them looked quite inspired,' Merv said encouragingly.

'Jeezus, Merv,' I snapped, 'they were the warders sent to keep an eye on our non-existent audience.'

*

But it wasn't our lack of evangelical success, I think that's the phrase, that undid us. It was betrayal, pure and simple.

Merv took it badly. For a while, I worried he might do something silly. Then he went to stay with his mum, who helped him get a part-time job at Bunnings. Apparently, his knowledge of sheds was a real asset.

When finally I caught up with him, he said, 'There's only one thing to say. Barry was a fucking prick. You hear that. A fucking prick! And we – you and I, that is – were so fucking foolish it's flabbergasting.' He grinned. 'Not bad, eh?'

'Smooth as,' I said, 'I'm really glad something good came out of this.'

Like Merv, the deceit hit me hard. For months, I could not say a single word to anyone, except when I went to the bottle shop. I simply could not believe that those I loved would do such a thing, could not believe my own blindness.

The signals were there, I just didn't see them. Didn't understand the significance of that day, not long before his release, when Barry and I both had visitors. His was a fine-looking woman, clearly not his mother. Mine was Fi, who'd just got out. She looked fantastic.

'Who's that big bloke over there staring at me, us?' she asked.

'That's our leader, Barry,' I said proudly. I'd told her as much as I dared to in a prisoner-to-prisoner letter about our plans.

'He's a fine-looking specimen,' she smiled. She sighed deeply. 'It'll be so good to have a project.'

'You still got your chemistry textbooks?' I asked.

'Somewhere,' she replied. 'My mother never throws anything out.'

Back in the cells that day, Barry declared, 'I saw the woman of my dreams today. Can't wait to spend time with her.'

'You're a lucky man,' I said affectionately. 'Only two weeks to go.'

'Thirteen days,' he corrected.

Then, his release, Fi's release, and an agonising silence. Finally that postcard, from Napa Valley of all places.

I have it in my hand right now as I wait for my flight to America.

Did they really think I'd just forgive and forget? Barry's change of name was as nasty a taunt as they come. But it inspired me afresh, gave me a sense of purpose as never before.

My KPI is crystal clear – destroying Phyll & Fi's wine bar and grill. From what I hear, the gas supply in San Francisco is quite accident prone.

A grieving mother writes

Dear Amanda

Do you remember the Lucas family, Freddie and Jean? They lived just down the road from us. They had two children, a boy of about eight and a little girl of three. She died. I think it was meningitis, though at the time we were more interested in chasing boys than in the names of childhood diseases. It was the night you and I went parking with those two guys at Long Reef – can't even remember their names. When I got home, it wasn't all that late, Mum was still awake. Dad was away on business. I had this bizarre conversation with her. She was obviously concerned about my sex life, particularly that I might have one. So she's talking, very Louisa style, about 'necking' and 'petting'. She actually used those terms, it was such a scream. And I'm standing there trying to pretend innocence, though I was pretty tousled.

Then Mum says, out of nowhere, 'Oh, by the way, the little Lucas girl died tonight.' Just like that. The question of whether I'd been groped or whatever was much more important than the shattering of our neighbour's life.

I remember so clearly how Freddie changed. His hair went white, a sort of yellowy white actually, his skin became grey and papery and seemed to hang off him. And he shuffled. I'll never forget the way he shuffled around the streets, even when he had a suit on and needed to catch the bus. Jean seemed to deal with it better, although it was hard to tell. She was always quiet. She got very fat, like a full, ripe, silent plum about to burst.

When I looked at them, I wondered how they could give up like that. As though someone had turned on a tap and their life juices just dribbled away.

I know now. God, I know. That sense of hopelessness, that anger, that rage inside you. Is it an instinct or an emotion? Does it lie in all of us, dormant, just biding its time? Did Freddie and Jean feel rage? They didn't seem to show it. Maybe they didn't get past hopelessness.

I started dreaming about this long row of stakes in the ground. Every one of them had a big label on it: shock, disbelief, anguish, horror, defeat, hopelessness, futility, bitterness, anger and so on. I had to collect all those labels just like harvesting a crop.

Oh, the images were so clear, gives me the shivers just writing about it now.

I knew what I had to do, though. My feet were bleeding, I didn't have any shoes on. I felt sick and hollow, I couldn't stop crying. But I forced myself along that row. I didn't miss a single label.

That dream was the only way I could purge my grief – and become just another wounded human being.

Yesterday and tomorrow

Names don't matter in this story. It could be that of many.

A year after they married, a baby was born. A wondrous child with a full round face, he smiled life back at them. They would gaze upon him, feeling a wonder and contentment they had never imagined possible.

Then, without warning, the baby died. One moment he was sleeping peacefully in his cot. A little later when the mother went to check on him, anticipating the surge of love which came each time she did this, their son had turned a colour that would stain her mind forever.

The father was outside their small house, some distance away. He heard a noise and looked up to see the mother running towards him, a bundle in her arms. The slope was in her favour and she was moving quite fast.

Then he heard her cry, an invocation, a plea from deep within. 'Our baby, our baby, our baby!' She passed the bundle to him.

He looked with horror upon their once-beautiful boy, now corrupted by an evil blue.

For many months, they moved as if in a blur, surrounded by a swirling mist of grief and compassion. They struggled to recall all the words, all the tears, showered on them and their little boy.

They would hear him in the house and startle to his cries. Then they would remember. He had been, he had gone, everything about him was in the past tense now.

They dreaded the nights. The house blazed with light when all about was dark. She took tablets, he opened another bottle. Lying on the bed where their little boy began, longing for unconsciousness, they occasionally made love in his memory.

Always the nightmares patrolled, awaiting their slumber.

The mother roamed in a world in which the only colour was blue. Sky, earth, water, fire, people, all were blue. When the moon rose at night, its misting blue light brushed casually against blue trees. A small blue boy followed her every move with his large blue eyes, his iridescent blue lips silently mouthing a single word, 'Mummy, Mummy, Mummy.'

The father would see her running towards him again, that same neat bundle sheltered in her arms. She cried out but was inaudible. Then she tossed the bundle high into the air and it came towards him in a long, gracious arc. He reached out with both arms but over his head it flew, quickly became a speck, then disappeared into the faraway hills, now constantly shrouded in blue.

This was their life, their condemned life, hostage to that evil day. Then came the miracle of another child. She was not a replacement, that could never be. But now they had no choice but to think of the days to come.

My island home

On the day of his release, I travelled to the dusty town where he and the others were 'admitted back into society'. By late afternoon, we were all on the same flight back to the capital, the forty ex-prisoners who had been out of it for more than a decade, the dozen or so journalists who had been away since that morning. We were like business people taking the trip home. Except that when the plane landed, the journalists caught taxis back to familiar places. They went to fractured new beginnings.

About two months later, I was walking near my home when I saw him coming towards me.

'I think I know you from the ceremony,' he greeted me softly.

It struck me as a curious way of describing that day. So began our friendship which led to the publication of my stories. I say 'my' stories but of course they were his. I was picking over his life. He was the one on display, the one taking risks.

He looked dishevelled the first time I called. I wondered if he had been asleep.

'It's good of you to drop by,' he said quietly, putting a large mug of warm tea in front of me.

We chatted. He asked how long I had been in the capital, whether I was alone; the usual inquiries of first acquaintance. I learned that his family had come to the house many years before. During the time he was away – he smiled as he said that – various friends had lived there.

After a while, I asked, 'What was it like on the island?'

He said nothing for what seemed an eternity. In the humid mid-afternoon stillness, I heard a clock chime four.

Finally, he said, 'I've been waiting for that question.'

Before he could say anything more, I said, quickly and self-consciously, 'I'd like to record this, if that's all right. I don't want to get you into trouble.'

He gave me a sad smile and shook his head. 'My friend, my young friend, you must understand this. For fourteen years, I could not be with those who were the core of my life. My wife fell ill, and when she died, her friends, not her husband, buried her. The news of that terrible event reached me many weeks later. Soon after, my children left. Perhaps without their mother's shelter, the stigma of their father's fate became too much to bear. Perhaps they simply despaired of ever seeing me again.' His voice wavered, then he continued. 'For fourteen years, my life belonged to someone else. What trouble can you cause me now?'

I felt my face redden with embarrassment.

Our first meeting lasted more than five hours. After four hours, I ran out of tape and scribbled furiously. I saw him a couple of times over the next few weeks but only briefly and it was another two months before we talked again at length.

That day when I arrived at his house, I noticed a policeman standing over the road.

'I have had other visitors since you were here last,' he said, ushering me into the living room.

The way he said 'visitors' alarmed me. 'Should we stop?' I asked.

To my guilty relief, he replied, 'How would that help?'

I left at nightfall. There were two policemen now. Both lit cigarettes at the very moment I went out the front gate and I saw their faces clearly. They said nothing but I could feel their eyes lasered on my back as I walked away.

One day, he said, 'You remember the guard I told you about. The one who confiscated the photograph I carried with me?'

'Yes,' I replied.

'I saw him terribly upset one morning. I heard there had been trouble in one of the outlying areas and one of his brothers, a policeman, had been killed. I thought about those two men for a long, long time. They served those I regarded as worse than unworthy. Had this tainted

52

them and stained all others in their family? Should I have quietly re-joiced at the death of the policeman or comforted the guard?'

'What did you do?'

'Nothing,' he replied, shaking his head. 'I could not decide, so to my shame I did nothing.

'Shame?'

'That guard was kind to me after my wife died.'

That day as I left, he said, 'I have something for you.' It was a copy of the photograph he had spoken about.

My articles were published over several days. I took great pride in the eloquence with which I told his story but wondered if it was not a dreadful conceit. After all, my own words were little more than binding for his testimony.

Five of us were taken before a judge. He was clean-shaven, with an oval face, and reminded me uncannily of one of my students. What if he were, I wondered? Would that have made it better or worse for me, or for him? I was amazed to find myself trying to remember what marks I had given that particular student.

In those first months, we itched for detail. We longed to know what was happening to us, why we had been detained, why we were sent to the island. Knowing would not have changed anything but it would have helped to define us as individuals. We quickly understood how easy it is to lose one's bearings in a factless environment.

After I had been on the island a few years, a small number of prisoners were released, or at least transferred. We did not begrudge them freedom, if indeed that was their fate. But we had, it seemed, all fused into a single being and it was agony when they were torn from us.

Not long after, one of the younger prisoners stole the small boat the guards used to patrol the island. A little way offshore, the engine cut out. That was how we discovered that every evening the guards removed the fuel tank in the boat and replaced it with one filled with water. We knew then what it was like to be a small bird or perhaps a mouse caught by a cat; any hope of escape was a taunt. We never saw that young man again.

Eight of us lived in a rough, cramped hut. One night, one of the men told a story, the next night another. Soon we were all taking turns. Then one of the men fell ill, so sick he was taken away. The sight of him lying on a canvas stretcher looking worn and frightened made me very uneasy. Yet we had to admit that his departure was convenient because our stories could now rotate with the week. We began, a little awkwardly at first, to call each other only by the name of our day, 'Tuesday', 'Friday', and so on. The other prisoners naturally became curious. One of them suggested that everyone assume a new name, and the idea was taken up enthusiastically. We had appropriated the days of the week so the others became a date. When the last of the prisoners was renamed '14 November', we could calculate, for the first time, exactly how many of us were on the island.

The most gifted of our storytellers was 'Thursday'. He was small and softly spoken but held our attention effortlessly. As 'Wednesday', I could feel the men's anticipation of the next evening as I tried to entertain them. Sometimes, Thursday amused us and we would wake next morning strangely refreshed. But I best remember this story.

It was a hot, shrivelled day towards the end of summer. An old woman was walking back to her village. She sat down to rest in the shade of a large, rambling tree and to her surprise heard the sound of a car coming slowly along the potholed road. A large black vehicle, its polished chrome fittings dazzling in the sunlight, eased around the corner.

She made herself as inconspicuous as possible but the car came to a halt, a tinted window half-opened and a voice called to her, 'Please, it is not a day for walking. Come with us.'

She was intrigued but uncertain.

'Come now,' the voice continued, more authoritatively. The driver got out. He was dressed in a smart brown uniform and wore the finest pair of boots the old woman had ever seen. He walked around and opened the door for her.

Still hesitating, she climbed in. As they neared her village, the driver asked for directions. A small, curious crowd watched as they pulled up outside her cottage. The woman's son looked on. The driver stepped out and opened the door. She offered demure thanks and the car slid away. Later that evening, they heard it passing through the village but it did not stop.

An odd thing now happened. Every week, on exactly the same day and at the same time, the car would pass through the village. Several of the older inhabitants observed that the car's outward travel was always at the same time but its return journeys were progressively quicker. They concluded that the car was visiting each of the villages along the mountain road. The car's passage became not just anticipated but welcomed. The village children and quite a few adults would stand by the side of the road waving and cheering. Some held up placards with VISIT US SOON or DON'T FORGET ABOUT US written carefully in eye-catching colours. A committee, led by the local schoolteacher, was formed to ensure that the visitors, whoever they were, received a fitting welcome. The streets were swept and the walls of the public buildings whitewashed. An air of expectation hung over the village and children tossed in their beds at night.

Then, one week, the car slowed and nosed straight to the home of the old woman. She filled with pride to see it standing right outside her small dwelling. The driver got out and once more she admired those boots. He opened both rear doors and stood to attention as two men alighted, one in a dark uniform. The children burst into their well-rehearsed song of welcome.

But even before they finished, the man in the dark uniform spoke to the old woman. 'Where is your son, madam?'

The boy, in his late teens, stepped out of the crowd, a smirk on his face at being singled out.

The man looked at him and with a jerk of his thumb barked, 'Into the car, you!'

A hush fell over the crowd.

'What?' the boy asked, surprise and wariness on his voice.

'You heard me. Into the car, I said!'

The driver and the man in civilian clothes now stood each side of the boy, grasping his arms.

The old woman had turned very pale. 'What do you want with him?' she asked, her voice trembling.

'We want nothing with him,' the man in the uniform said shrugging his shoulders. 'But we knew where you lived. It saved time having to find someone else.'

'What has he done, though?' she asked in a high voice, repeating the question several times.

'Done? Done!' The uniformed man seemed incredulous. 'We'll think of something.' He looked at the other man and the driver.

The three of them smirked.

Soon after that day, the old woman saw her son's name on a list, published by the authorities, of those helping 'To suppress elements seeking to undermine the state'. That was as close as she ever came to her son again.

There was a heavy silence after Thursday finished. Slowly the men began to speak.

'Stupid, naive villagers,' one said.

'They were trusting, that's all,' another remarked.

'Set up by their committee, that's what,' a third commented.

'Maybe the committee was taken in too,' said a fourth man.

'Then what was the point of having an educated man as its leader?' the third man retorted.

I could feel all eyes on me.

*

A week after my articles appeared, he vanished. I was sickened at the thought of what I had done. Difficult months passed. I was desperate to find him. There was no logical path of family or friends that might help me, and for the first time I truly understood just how much he had been dispossessed. But he had mentioned the names of a few other prisoners. I was wary of approaching them directly, guilty perhaps about my likely role in his disappearance. I wrote to them and received two replies. One thanked me warmly for telling his story. But the tone of the other response was sharp and accusatory. I was a meddler in a situation I could never truly comprehend.

One day, I received a phone call requesting me to meet with a senior government official, someone I knew and respected, though cautiously. I took this summons as a hopeful sign. Notions of justice attained and friendship renewed ran through my head. My efforts and his courage had revealed the truth of that terrible time. We had challenged those in power to confront what had been done in the name of the state and, in a few cases no doubt, to consider their own actions. We had forged a new beginning.

How breathlessly naive were those thoughts, those dreams. The meeting lasted less than ten minutes. I was invited to sit but, contrary to usual courtesies, no refreshments were offered. The official spoke from a written script. It condemned me for reopening old wounds, for my unacceptable behaviour. I was given one week to get my affairs in order and leave the country.

There was only one affair that truly mattered. He had told me of a beach on the island, the memory of which was one of the few joys he took from all those years of dislocation. I travelled to the island and found the beach, a small strip of the finest golden sand washed by clear, turquoise water which had soothed scabbed and aching feet. As the sun edged towards the horizon, I gathered debris from above the waterline and lit a small fire. When its flame was hot and pure, I knelt and burnt the photograph he had given me. It dissolved into a pale blue trace that left the island far behind, forever. The photograph showed three young men, their arms over each other's shoulders, smiling broadly at the camera. They were happier times, when these men were brothers – not a guard and a policeman and a highly educated prisoner of the state.

I sat there for some time then rose slowly and walked into the ocean. The waves began to buffet then wash over me. I pushed on. He had escaped the island but I had destroyed his freedom. I would make amends in the only way I could. The island would hold me forever. I kept walking.

No one is safe from the past

1

When Joshua was seven years old, he and his schoolfriends were taken to see a film about Nazi atrocities against the Jews. His parents had argued about whether he join the group.

'He's so young,' his mother Miriam pleaded. 'Let him be a boy a little longer.'

'He should go,' his father Ariel declared. 'We cannot protect him from the past. He needs to understand the world he lives in.'

'There'll be time for that,' Miriam argued. 'We'll know when he is ready.'

The discussion went on acrimoniously for several hours.

Next day, Ariel insisted on dropping Joshua to school, waiting with him until he boarded the bus with the other children.

When Joshua arrived home later that day, he was quieter than usual.

Miriam felt vindicated. 'Are you all right, darling?' she asked.

He nodded and smiled carefully at her. His young mind simmered but he lacked the words to convey the two things that haunted him most about the film. One was the lonely, rolling whistle of the trains transporting the condemned. The other was the mist that seemed constantly to lace the unfolding tragedy.

'We should not have done that to him,' Miriam said firmly to Ariel that night.

'Done what?' asked Ariel. 'He's always been a quiet boy.'

'I want him to lead a normal life,' said Miriam.

'The blessing and the curse of our people,' Ariel replied. 'is that we can never have one.'

A few weeks after seeing the film, Joshua was on an outing with his father, a misty winter's evening in Jerusalem with softened landscapes and sharpened footfalls. Suddenly, in the distance, he heard the whistle of a train. The film replayed in his mind. He need not be alarmed, he told himself. Such trains are no more. Yet that one single sound, shrouded in white and echoing into the hills, carried such a message both of death and the manner of dying that Joshua visibly trembled.

His father looked at him, puzzled.

Back home, his parents tried to comfort him, struggling to understand Joshua's blubbering explanation of his new-found fear of trains.

2

I have no name, for I am not yet born, fresh seeded by the love between Yasmin and Yacov. A dangerous tie, it fills their hearts with joy and dread and makes them furtive and alert. Like cats, which Yasmin sees as she glides across Jerusalem, its past heavy on the air. Her two friends trail in her wake, savouring their role in this romance of the night.

'Darling Yasmin,' said her friends one day as they waited for the anonymity of dusk, 'your secret world is safe with us though we fear the path you've chosen.'

Yasmin hugged them, murmuring, 'This path chose me.'

She is a brave or foolish girl, my mother of tomorrow.

*

'When first we met,' she once said to her lover, 'I could not believe in you. A kind and gentle Jew contradicted all I had been told.'

Yacov smiled and kissed her hand. 'And you,' he said with wonderment, 'are you truly of those people? These fingers do not taste of hate.'

They were silent for a time then Yasmin said, 'The art of hatred must be learned and we must disappoint our teachers.'

*

In Yasmin's home, I hear the voices of her brothers and their father. Bitter voices plotting vengeance for wrongs sharp in recollection though the details are forgotten. Once, but only once, I heard her protest at the vileness of their words.

Her brothers looked at her and said in unison, 'What would a woman know!'

She sat in silence, weeping at their scorn.

Now Yasmin's mother cries long into the night for a son who will not return. The father and the others sit with muffled pride as neighbours come to celebrate his martyrdom.

'He killed many of the enemy today,' the youngest brother proclaims, as if the merit of this deed shimmers on them all.

The father adds, although with stricken voice, 'He brought great honour to our family and will long be remembered.'

*

Yacov's heart lies heavy in his chest when next he meets Yasmin. 'My friend has met a terrible death,' he says.

'I know your grief,' Yasmin replies and holds him near. She makes no mention of her brother, the martyr and killer of the friend.

*

There is tension in the home, for Yasmin has returned later than is wise.

'Where have you been?' her brother Nabil asks.

'I have been walking,' she says. Her voice is anxious but defiant.

'With whom?'

She is surprised by the question. 'With my dear friends. You know them well.'

Nabil is not silenced. 'Who else?' he demands.

I feel her nervousness.

Still, calmly she says, 'We greeted some others. Is that wrong?'

'Enough, Nabil,' the father says. 'Her friends are worthy of our trust. Do not be late again,' he gently warns his daughter.

*

Hardly does she take his hand than Yacov says determinedly, 'We have
to stop!'

Yasmin's face floods with surprise and hurt. 'But why?' she pleads.

'We have been foolish,' he says, 'believing we could shape our lives
without heed of yesterday. There is too much blood on all our hands.'

'Then we must try to wash it off,' she cries.

'Tell that to your brothers!' Yacov's voice is acid-bitter, as if he and
they are one.

*

Yasmin knows now I grow within. Terrified yet overjoyed, she writes to
Yacov.

I weep as I remember those glances and answered looks. One day
you gave me sign, and I came to you across the chasm of the past, moving as the air through time-flavoured streets. We knew then, did we
not, that we were the new chosen ones? Afterwards, I stroked your cool,
unblemished nakedness. Why is it I asked that we have melted together,
soft and smooth as liquid, yet beyond us all is roughed and bleeding?

You lay there for a time then said, 'History is a coarse sandpaper.'

My two companions waited, their loyalty tainted with embarrassment. 'How could you?' they asked as we walked home.

'But there is good between us,' I replied.

'He is a Jew,' they said.

'And I am not, so which of us is lesser?'

'He stole our land,' they said.

'Did Yacov steal our land or those before him? We cannot curse and
kill forever.'

My friends grew quiet, mystified at my forgiveness.

She longs to tell Yacov of me but cannot find the words.

*

Coming to the table with telltale eyes, Yacov eats in gloomy silence until his father, with Yacov's friend in mind, declares, 'Our sadnesses must make us strong or else they have no purpose.'

Yacov asks uncertainly, 'Is it possible to both love and hate the other side?'

'Anything is possible,' the father says, surprised, 'but why risk such confusion?'

*

Nabil is at the door, dismissing Yasmin's friends. 'She will not be going with you tonight. She is coming with her brothers.'

Startled by this pronouncement, Yasmin tries to speak.

'You will do as we say,' Nabil declares. The air is sharp with nicotine and smoke flutters from his nostrils.

Three other brothers file into the room trying not to look at her.

'Come!' Nabil says.

Yasmin's father hugs her swiftly and she sees his eyes are wet. She hears her mother in the other room, gasping, as for the perished son.

They drive through a blurring landscape and, for one frightened, desperate moment, Yasmin thinks their destination is the father of her child. She trembles at the thought of such a meeting. But when the vehicle stops, there are no lights nearby. The door is opened and a hand is firmly on her elbow. She walks unsteadily across a rock-strewn field filled with gentle moon.

The brothers form a circle round Yasmin and one of them says savagely, 'You lover of the Jew, you shame us all!'

The soft night air washes his words away as Nabil reaches inside his coat. The knife blade glints as it arcs towards my mother's belly.

Beware of gospel fine print

Ingathering

No more coy glances across the pews, for I'm in her bed at last, white-hot with hunger as she arches her back, breathing hard, an animal pant from deep inside which urges me on and my stiff cock is crazy with desire when the door bursts open and two men dressed in black trousers and frilled white shirts rush into the room and one of them shoots her right between the eyes, no mean feat given his thrashing target and I wonder, absurdly, whether he might have trained as a marksman or even for the Olympics.

But this is not the moment for such unhinged deliberation, as these two men now grab my stammering legs and drag me to the floor, sniggering at my rapidly withered malehood, and I am shocked to recognise them as fellow congregants who often sat close by in Temple, though at this particular moment their names float only on the outskirts of my frenzied mind.

One slaps me hard across the face and my spinning head then spins with all of me as I am rolled into the carpet I had much admired when first she brought me to this fine apartment, saying with a smile it was her father's residence reserved for special Bible studies, upon which she did not elaborate, but I imagined exquisite moments on this textile now fashioned into a cylinder in which, terrified and breathing motes, I am lugged downstairs.

Dumped heavily on an unforgiving surface, I hear a door slide shut followed by two duller closings and as we start to move there is a faint groan right beside me and even in my fuddled state I know the sound of another human being in large distress but in my carpet swaddle, arms pinioned at my sides, all I can do is wriggle until I bump into another thing which bumps me back and we bump and bump and bump like some archaic mating, far from the delicious swoon I had anticipated such short time ago.

Blinded and smothered as we are, there can be no other communication and my desperate mind now casts around for little shards of memory which might sustain me – the time our hands first brushed in Temple, her mysterious family outings, the invitation whispered in my ear – but I cannot hold such images long and soon I am alone, drifting in a rough wooden boat on a broad grey ocean, terribly parched and sunburnt until suddenly I'm awakened, possibly by the horror of that image but more likely because a siren has jagged the vehicle and pulled it magnet-like to the edging of the road.

Where a conversation which might just have offered rescue takes place between our captors and those they keep referring to as sir, or, of course sir, or, understand entirely officer, and I join the conversation though not on the polite and grovelling terms with which it's being conducted oh-so-close but by yelling out my lungs as much as my soured mouth and carpet coffin will allow and my fellow-bumpers soon follow suit and joy-oh-joy I hear the magic words, what's going on inside the van boys, then the voices muffle but I still catch their drift and the words, why that's a generous sum, lads, just promise that you won't disturb the neighbours with whatever game you're playing with your friends in there, and, sure thing, sarge, you can rely on us, all make clear there'll be no salvation and then our vehicle grumbles into life and draws away with us near-suffocated beings quivering in its belly.

Nothing for hours except the rattle of the road until there comes the ticking of an engine cooling and a squeaking, crunching noise like metal wheels shoved hard on gravel then the van door sliding open and shouts and we the cargo dragged onto a cart and so it seems we have arrived.

Adjudication

Rough hands reach in and manacle my ankles and suddenly I am winched feet first into the spinning air, the cause of this wild sensation being also that I am peeled of my carpet skin like an onion being delayered, though with the residue of recent events upon me, I dare not lay a claim to an aroma near as sweet.

We are in a barn-like building and three of us, naked as the day we made our entry into this sharp world and with a cruel white light upon us, hang feet-first from a metal pipe held up at each end by stout trestles while a little away sit three others and, horrified, I know the truth that there's nothing random about this encounter for we are all of the very same congregation and the old man who sits with malevolent appearance is not just the father of the one so recently executed in my arms but of the two who caused such wretched amorous interruptus and brought me to this place.

Metronomic-like, the old man's eyes sweep back and forth as if anxious not to miss a single moment of the play and, making the sign of the cross, he speaks, his voice starched with menace as he reads the scroll, fresh-penned it seems, his two sons hold aloft. 'Bless us, Lord, for we are gathered in Thy sight as upholders of those ancient texts which make clear the order of Your grand universe and the place of male and female, decreeing not just that the father is the superior being within the home but that the firstborn daughter will be given to him and to any sibling males and if an interloper offends upon such ordinance he shall be brought to justice swift and true and these perverted souls swinging before us have done You great offence by sullying our daughter-sister whom we had much enjoyed and who it pained us sore to have removed from further taint by those foul souls stretched before us who, as is Your wont, will soon be cleansed from this cherished earth for the nearing end of days.'

As my brain picks feebly at these words, one of my fellow-danglers cries out, but she loved me and I her, and I am torn between true admiration for the courage of such declaration and a pepper sting of jealousy that he most likely had known a pleasure denied to me so wantonly at the very moment of fulfilment, but as I turn towards the speaker, one of the sons, with a knowing look from the father, wraps plastic film around his head and pulls it tight and I watch aghast the ugly purpling of the poor man's face and his breath receding until it stutters to a gentle calm.

The old man shakes his head almost as if regret has come upon him but when he speaks his voice floods with derision for those who he declares did not sufficiently attend to the wording of the gospels which makes clear that the fate of women is for their fathers and their brothers only to decide as long has been the custom and, though the Temple now stands tall and sleek as any modern symbol, the ancient ways must still hold sway and those who dare to flout them, female or male, will find their breath foreshortened in ways no witting soul would ever seek.

The resignation of the condemned not the valour of the living within me, I yell, why now, and the old man looks at me with eyebrows lifted and says, you cursed beings, she was with child and one of you may well have been the father, which by the very gospels studied close in Temple cannot be allowed, so we have mustered you to exact the retribution of the Lord.

Upside down is no good place to beg one's case and tears leak across my forehead as I cry but we are fellow congregants and derelict perhaps in our devotions – for I do not know the special passages to which he has referred – everything that happened was between the people of the Temple and all of us, his and our (my) poor dead darling too, acted as free beings to which the old man sneers, God's will is never free and He demands a vengeance for your vile liberation of my daughter, thus robbing me of what I rightly owned.

We are not owners of each other and can never be, I plead, but then my face is slapped so hard that blood and mucus leak inside my head and the old man yells, Enough! a cry which spins around the barn, piercing my petrified soul, and we hang there silent, dribbling from our orifices.

Correction

The old man glistens with contempt then gazes to a corner of the room where large smooth stones lie neatly piled, but eventually he shakes his head and declares, we will not waste the precious weapon of the scriptures upon these evil-doers for a body that is crushed allows the spirit to fly free and it behoves us to contain such evil, then, cupping his hands, he reaches into a pail and splashes water upon himself and his two sons while uttering an incantation unbeknown to me.

And so with frozen tongue and bleating eye, cursing the day I joined the Temple and my abjuration of the fine print of the gospels, and forlornly, uselessly, begging her forgiveness for my wanton blindness, hypnotised I watch the preacher and his male spawn, plastic-armed, advance towards us carcasses-in-waiting.

God's honest truth

Once upon a time in a little place that nobody really cared about, a terrible thing happened. Some nasty men found some good men trying to prove their goodness by showing just how nasty the others were. The nasty men killed the good men. Everyone said that was truly nasty. Everyone, that it, except the good men who couldn't speak any more because they were dead. But that only went to show how good they really were.

Then a funny thing happened. Lots of people began to point their fingers at the king, saying, 'You should have told those nasty men not to kill those good men. You didn't, so you must be a nasty king.'

The king was puzzled and indeed a little hurt. He said out loud, 'I told the nasty men not to be so nasty. But if I'd told them about the good men, they would have killed them even quicker.'

Few believed the king and some cried out, 'You knew those good men were there and you didn't do anything about it. What's the point of having you as our king? No one takes any notice of you, especially us.'

The king tried one more time. 'But the good men didn't tell me where they were going. I had no idea they were there. God's honest truth.'

'Oh, pull the other one!' someone yelled and the people booed the king and threw apples and rotten eggs at him.

'We knew everything that happened,' said one of their leaders, 'so you must too.'

'But I didn't, I truly didn't,' pleaded the king as his courtiers led him back inside the palace. There, they had an intense discussion that went on for many years.

Outside, they could hear the people muttering and cursing and some of them calling the king a liar and a cheat. They even said that if he loved the nasty people that much, he should go and live with them and let everyone else get on with the business of being good which they did so well. One small girl wrote to the king saying she wanted to be the goodest person in the world but didn't see how she could while he was still king. The king showed the letter to his wife that night and they were both very upset.

'I know you're a good man, dear,' the queen said, 'but sometimes it all gets a bit confusing. Not everyone understands that.'

'Tell me about it,' said the king, which was an usual thing for him to say and showed just how upset he was.

The next day, the king had another meeting with his courtiers.

One of the clever ones said, 'The problem, your majesty, is that some of the people think you're hiding something. They say you knew what was going to happen to those good men and did nothing to stop it.'

'That's preposterous!' said the king. 'I did not know what was going to happen and anyway why would I have behaved like that?'

'Maybe you didn't like the good men,' chirped another courtier, who everyone thought was a bit too smart for his own good.

The king scowled at him. 'What should I do now?' the king asked the clever courtier.

'Well, your majesty, have you ever thought of writing a book?'

'What about?'

'About everything you know.'

The too-smart-for-his-own-good courtier just stopped himself from saying the book would not be very long. Instead he said, 'That's a great idea, your majesty, a wonderful gift to your people.'

The king smiled and nodded.

In the springtime, the king held a big garden party and invited everyone to see his new book. It was in fact longer than all the books in the kingdom put together and everyone was impressed.

'How brilliant you are!' the courtiers cried, clapping their hands almost as one.

The king made a brief speech saying he was sorry for all the confusion and misunderstanding about what had happened to the good men all that while ago. 'I've revealed all I know,' he said, 'except one or two little bits and pieces that wouldn't be of any interest to anyone, God's honest truth.'

'Aha! I told you. That's always the giveaway,' a short fat whiskery man in the crowd said to his friend.

She nodded agreement. They went away and wrote a story for the newspaper and said the king was 'covering up'. Just in case someone thought that meant the king was cold, they went on to explain he was not telling the truth.

'The king's a liar!' one boy told his friend next day, after hearing his parents discussing the story over breakfast.

When the king saw the story, he was very angry. But the clever courtier said that even if he hadn't told everything, he was still an honest man and should act like one. He whispered something to the king and the next day the whiskery man and his friend, to their considerable surprise, found themselves invited to the palace for lunch.

Barely had they sat down, however, than they said in unison, 'We know you're hiding something.'

The king was very calm and asked, 'What am I hiding?'

The two guests looked at each other. They knew this was a tricky question.

'Well, if we knew that, you wouldn't be hiding it any more would you!' one of them said, sounding exasperated.

'You mean I have to tell you what you think is the truth,' the king said slowly, 'and then I won't be hiding it any more?'

'That's about it,' the short whiskery man said with a grin.

'Well, what do you need to hear?' asked the king.

'This!' the short man said brusquely. He told an awful story about what had happened to the good men. But as he spoke, his friend began to look puzzled, so puzzled in fact that the king interrupted and asked, 'Are you all right?'

'I suppose so,' she replied, still quite distracted. Then she turned to the whiskery man and said quietly, 'But that's not what happened. I'm sure it was like this –'

The whiskery man cut her short. 'You know as well as I do that –'

They began to argue fiercely and forgot entirely about the king, who slipped out of the room.

'What do I do now?' he asked the clever courtier.

'Nothing,' came the reply. 'Let them squabble for as long as they like. And when they finish, ask them how you can be expected to know the truth if they don't. That will keep them quiet.'

'You are a clever one,' said the king, a big smile on his face, 'and that's God's honest truth.'

A greater good for some

After so many years of attending other people's funerals, it was such a relief finally to be at my own. My departure, though, was a real disappointment. Only now do I truly comprehend the term 'slipped away'. I'd hoped to make more of statement. Like Beethoven, shaking his fist at the thunder and lightning. Well, I guess it was more the lightning, as he couldn't hear the thunder. Way to go, Ludwig!

I was chuffed that quite a few people seemed put out. There'd be nothing worse than dying and no one really noticing. You can imagine the sort of thing. Someone asks after you. 'Oh, you didn't know? He/she died three years ago, must have forgotten to tell you. Goodness, how time flies.'

There was a decent turn-up for the cremation too, but just one problem. I'm sure I left written instructions that I wanted to be buried, dust-to-dust sort of thing. I'm not saying my wishes were deliberately flouted. Maybe in the stress of the moment someone just forgot. I won't hold that against them. But I won't forgive the 'No Flowers by Request'. Whose request, I'd bloody well like to know! It certainly wasn't mine. I love flowers, especially at final farewells. Those big white velvety lilies with their heady aromas, the gorgeous yellows and reds and blues of the supporting cast. I used to pop into funerals just to see the flowers. Didn't matter that I'd never laid eyes on the deceased.

Funny to think that I'm in that category now.

Anyway, there I was, flowerless and quite pissed off. But there's not much you can do when you're dead. That's one of its downsides.

I'd tried to lead a decent life, at least no worse than most others. Which naturally raises the big question. Where to? Well, rather to my surprise, I drifted upwards. I don't know how much time elapsed, as my watch didn't survive the crematorium. I just arrived 'there'. One of the first things I noticed was that everyone was wearing a black armband. Seemed odd.

'Excuse me, Henry,' I asked, 'what's the story with the armbands. Thought they'd be redundant around here.'

Apologies, I should have explained. All new arrivals get a minder to show them the ropes. Mine's Henry. Nice chap, though he seems a bit prone to mood swings. A trainee priest, he was run over by a horse and cart about eight hundred years ago. Still, he's very up to date, a real whiz on the computer.

'A most regrettable situation, I'm afraid,' Henry replied. 'One I never believed could happen in my lifetime, excuse me, I meant deathtime.'

I could see by the look on his face he wasn't trying to be funny. I waited.

'Someone very special has passed on.'

'You mean died? But that's how we all got here.'

Henry chewed his lip. 'Not exactly. Think about it.' He stared at me.

'Oh no, you don't mean,' I gasped.

'I'm afraid so,' he said, looking crestfallen.

'Oh God, that's terrible.'

'Careful,' Henry warned. 'Even in the light of recent, um, unfortunate events, we should not be taking certain names in vain.'

'Sorry.'

'We will continue as before, making sure we practise our deep breathing,' Henry went on, a determined look on his face.

'But how, how can we, you? I mean –'

'There's been a contingency plan for quite some time.'

'I don't understand.'

'Well, a special Doomsday Committee will now take whatever decisions are required.' He paused then said, very deliberately, 'No one outside here need be any the wiser. Get it?'

'But that's cheating. Good people are dying just to sit on the right hand of someone who's no longer around. That doesn't seem fair.'

'Now listen,' Henry rebuked, 'you should be very careful about what you say and how you say it. It would be terrible, just terrible, if this news was to reach another place. Just imagine the gloating if our opponent were to learn of our misadventure. Right?'

I nodded, feeling sad and confused. We were silent for a bit, then Henry said, 'I wouldn't be surprised if the committee opts for a change of direction.'

'I take it you're on the committee?' I asked.

Henry ignored the question. 'There's a feeling we opened the gates too wide,' he went on. 'Remember, we started out with strict entry requirements, the Ten Commandments, the need to sort the sheep from the goats, et cetera. We capped total admissions at twenty-five thousand, upped it to seventy thousand and finally to a hundred and forty-four thousand. All eminently reasonable. Unfortunately, we then got into a silly competition with the other side, standards went out the window. There was even that advertising campaign – Where the bloody hell are you?'

'I didn't know that was about getting into Heaven,' I exclaimed. 'A clever play on words and a swipe at the opposition. Very neat.'

'I suppose it was,' said Henry, 'but it got completely out of hand when we allowed McDonalds and that silly theme park to open.'

'You mean the garden of heavenly delights?' I chortled. 'I can't wait to have a look. It's one of the reasons I'm so glad I got in.'

'You're not here to sightsee!' Henry snapped. 'If you think you were accepted because of good behaviour, think again. We knew you had a marketing background.'

'What's wrong with that?'

'What's right with it would be a better question, but let's not worry about that now. The simple fact is we need to discourage people from wanting to get into Heaven. The fewer souls floating around here, the less the chance of an unfortunate leak about our circumstances.'

'How do I fit in?'

'We need to get some negative messages out.'

'But I never did any political advertising,' I said. 'I was strictly sales.'

'Look,' Henry said sharply, 'lots of people would die for an opportunity like this. You did. Your name came out in the lucky draw and the opportunity is yours. Do you really want me to tell the committee it scored a dud? The members will very disappointed. Very,' he repeated, sounding ominous. 'Now I can understand you might want a bit of time to think about it, but the committee –'

'No, no, no,' I broke in, thinking quickly. 'What about an FAQ?'

Henry looked at me blankly.

'Frequently asked questions,' I explained. 'They're always more authoritative than straight ads. I'll work on a draft overnight if you like.'

'Well, you better get to it!'

*

Henry seemed a bit more relaxed next morning.

'I've tried to keep it simple,' I said, 'concentrating on the things that matter most to people.'

'Go on,' he said.

'Okay. Question: is Heaven a land of milk and honey? Answer: a recent review found a serious problem of obesity and a strict diet of bread, water and apples is being introduced.'

'I like the apples,' Henry smiled, 'clever historical touch.'

'Question,' I continued, 'is alcohol permitted?'

'There'll be a lot of interest in this answer,' Henry said.

'Well, there are bound to be a few smarty pants quoting biblical passages about taking a little wine for their stomach's sake. They'll just have to put up with the new reality: non-alcoholic beers and wines are available after five p.m. every second Monday.'

Henry looked alarmed.

'Henry, Henry,' I calmed, 'the rule apply to newcomers only, not to us. Changes like this are always handled that way.'

Henry nodded. 'There's certainly no place for retrospectivity in Heaven. Next!'

'Is sex permitted? Answer: only for the specific purposes of old-style begatting. Or is it begotting? Maybe begetting? I was never really sure.'

'Doesn't matter,' said Henry dismissively. 'Great answer. It'll keep out most of the clergy and all of the LGBTQIA and so on and so forth. That's a real bonus. But,' he paused, 'some might argue that it's discriminatory.'

'I thought that was the whole point, Henry. Deter people banging on Heaven's gates.'

'It is, it is,' Henry conceded. 'Just feels somewhat,' he searched for the word, 'contradictory. After all, we've been running that line about universal love and kindness for a long time.'

'Come on Henry,' I said, 'you know as well as I do that was marketing, pure and simple! And very effective, too. Now, you've changed the product as it your right to do.'

'I can see why we wanted you here,' Henry nodded. 'Anything else?'

'Couple of things,' I said. 'We need particular messages targeted at women and those who want to fly.'

'I'm not with you,' he said.

'Well, there are quite a few high-profile women in the Bible, like Eve and Sarah and Rachel and Ruth and the Marys –'

'You know your Bible well,' he said admiringly. 'The point being?'

'We need to be careful about portraying Heaven as an equal opportunity destination. We shouldn't overdo the blokey image, particularly white blokes and I can see there's a good blend here, but the place shouldn't sound too modern and open-minded. That could be a real incentive for the wrong people to want to get in.'

'What do mean the wrong people?' Henry asked. 'Women?'

'Not just women, but anyone who might ask awkward questions. This is a place where people should do as they're told. By the committee, that's what it's for.'

'Goes without saying,' said Henry, 'but we better say it anyway. Find some words will you?'

'Sure,' I said. I was very pleased with the way this was all turning out. 'Last point, flying.'

'I'm intrigued,' said Henry.

'I'll bet a lot of those who've ended up here did it for the wings.'

'You're a bit late on that one,' Henry cautioned. 'There was a wing-distribution rort a while back. You-know-who dealt with it very harshly. Wrath with a capital W. Not a pretty sight, I can tell you.'

'Why not ban wings altogether?' I asked. 'You can say they cause arthritis, or they contribute to climate change, or that it's healthier to walk. Course it wouldn't affect those who already have them. Like you and the other committee members.'

'I like what I'm hearing,' said Henry. 'But you do realise there's a qualifying period for wings. If we ban them now you'll miss the cut.'

'Not a problem,' I said. 'It's about a greater good. Maybe the committee can reward me in some other way.'

'I'm sure we'll find something suitable,' Henry smiled.

'What I'm beginning to understand about this place,' I said, 'is that it's really like home. I can see why people are very keen to get in.'

'Funny you should say that,' Henry replied. 'There's a saying among the old-timers. Paradise on earth when you're down there. Earth in paradise when you're up here. Mind you, we were wary about talking too openly like that when someone who…' He stopped and shook his head. 'No. No. No. That would be disloyal. I won't say anything more.'

'No need to, Henry,' I said. 'I understand exactly where you're coming from. Old chapters end, new ones start. We're honouring the past and adjusting to changed circumstances.'

Henry nodded. 'I think I should nominate you for the committee.'

'It'd be a privilege,' I replied.

'Only for some,' he said with a smile.

The greatest game

And the people gathered together, grumbling among themselves. They approached the Lord, saying, 'Now don't get us wrong and we're really grateful for the way you got us out of Egypt. But quite frankly, things get a bit quiet in the desert, especially at the weekends.'

'What's your point?' asked the Lord.

'Well,' said the people, 'we wondered if we could invent some sort of game –'

'I'm the inventor around here,' the Lord reminded them sharply.

'Of course, of course,' said the people. 'Sorry. Perhaps You could create a game to provide carefree family entertainment and encourage a sense of team spirit among the young.'

'Let me sleep on it,' said the Lord. 'I'll let you know tomorrow.'

'Does the Lord really sleep too?' asked one little boy in the crowd.

'Shhh,' his mother warned.

The next morning, the gong sounded early and the people assembled promptly.

'Okay,' said the Lord, 'I've come up with a game called cricket. It'll be played over five days and will be called a test.'

'There He goes again,' muttered a middle-aged man in the crowd, 'always testing us. Can't He give us a break just for once? And five days, how ridiculous!'

'That's enough, dear,' soothed his wife.

'Here are the rules,' the Lord continued. 'I've had them carved into these stone tablets. Mind that you study them well.'

'Yes, Lord,' replied the crowd. 'Thank you Lord for cricket. We shall play it in Thy name.'

And they did. And they were content, and peace and healthy sporting attitudes bound the community closely together. But after a while, fresh grumbling could be heard.

'It's a silly game,' a few of the men said. 'It goes for so long and sometimes there's not even a winner and they call it a draw. What a stupid word. Or just occasionally, on the fourth or the fifth day, it gets a bit interesting and then there's a dust storm or maybe a flash flood and still there's no result.'

'But we asked for it in the first place,' some of the other men chided.

'We asked for something that would kill time, not drag it out endlessly.'

'Cricket is the Lord's work,' said its defenders.

The others fell silent. But only for a time. For the feeling that cricket wasn't all it might be gradually gained strength. Teams were hard to muster, very few turned up to training, and crowd attendances dropped sharply. A delegation of community elders was despatched to meet the Lord.

'What is it now?' He demanded.

'We thank You daily for all You have given us,' the delegation leader intoned. 'But,' he paused for a moment, 'the truth is that, um, cricket in its current form is not holding the community's attention.'

'And why not?' asked the Lord tetchily.

'Well, it goes for too long and often goes nowhere.'

'All right,' said the Lord, 'I'll see what I can do. Again,' he added, with heavy emphasis. 'But I really don't know how any of you will get into Heaven if you can't keep your mind on one thing even for a few days.'

'Thank you, Lord,' the delegation sighed in unison, anxious to be away.

'He's in a great mood,' one of them whispered sarcastically.

'Quiet!' the leader snapped. 'Haven't you heard of omniscience?'

'Oops, sorry. Do you think he might have –?'

'Forget it! Just watch your tongue.'

But the Lord was as good as His word. And so one-day cricket came to pass.

'Hallelujah, hallelujah,' the crowd cried out. 'God is the greatest and so is fifty overs-a-side cricket.'

Contentment lay across the community like a thick woollen blanket on a cold, clear night.

And then, amazingly, the rumbles of discontent started all over again.

'A whole day to watch one game. What a waste!'

'I could pick half my olive harvest by the time the game's finished!'

'The crowd behaviour's just disgraceful. Why don't they ban the sale of pomegranate juice at the grounds?'

So another delegation was despatched.

'What is it with you lot?' the Lord asked in exasperation. 'Can't you keep your mind on anything for more than five minutes?'

'No,' the delegation replied sheepishly.

'Lord, might it be possible to have a word in private?' asked the youngest member of the delegation, a handsome, clean-cut man in his early nineties.

'Well, I suppose so,' said the Lord, without enthusiasm. 'It better be good. What's your name?'

'Moses,' replied the man.

'Okay, Moses, see that hill over there. Be at the top at midnight.'

'Thank you, Lord.'

Next morning, as the people gathered around their campfires to cook breakfast, Moses appeared, a look of triumph on his tired face.

'Here at last is the answer,' he proclaimed, unfurling a chalk-white parchment.

The people gathered around and read aloud in wonderment.

One-One Cricket – the rules

Each side shall consist of twelve players, one of who shall be nominated as umpire; each side shall bowl a maximum of one over; no bowler shall bowl more than one ball; no batsman shall face more than one ball; the position of wicketkeeper shall rotate after each ball; whoever is wicket keeping shall assume the position of team captain; whenever the ball is hit, no matter how near or far, the batters must run; a ball hit to the boundary scores five runs, plus any additional ones run by the batsmen while the ball is being fielded; a ball hit over the boundary on the full scores ten runs, plus any additional ones run by the batsmen while the ball is being retrieved; balls hit to or over the boundary must be returned without delay by spectators.

As they finished reading, the people fell to their knees. 'Oh Lord, provider of all that is good, we give thanks for one-one cricket. Through it, you have ensured that never again will our interest wane or our concentration lapse.'

I wonder about that, thought the Lord. I really wonder.

But He kept his doubts to Himself.

When ball-kids go bad

It embarrasses me now to think how much of a goody-goody I was when I first started. Conscientious and anxious to please, guileless. Not like some of the other girls. They wore their innocence like a badge. But they also wore perfume and used words like cock, and even cunt, and wondered aloud about the size of the male stars' 'members'. They said that word slyly and it always produced a healthy snicker, even from newbies like me with shiny, naive faces.

To see us all in action, you wouldn't have guessed any of this. We looked so young and fresh and eager. Regimentally precise in what we did, catching and running and underarming balls to the back of the court and getting smartly into place. Crouching by the net, spring-loaded to dash off again. A model for all young people, one commentator remarked. Clearly, she hadn't heard of some of the Snapchat posts. These included one from a girl who claimed she'd souvenired one of Rafael Nadal's sweaty towels and slept on it every night. Naked.

I did believe in the worthy stuff for a while. I was pretty good at tennis and my parents nagged me for years to apply to be a ball-kid. The day we learnt I'd been selected for the Australian Open, they looked at me with tears in their eyes, praising my posture and athleticism, my maturity and determination. Words straight out of Tennis Australia's ball-kid manual. On the court, I looked sharp, fine-tuned. What parent wouldn't think of their kid as a member of an elite?

In my second year, I was a good as anyone with the lewd banter and winking smiles. My parents would have been shocked at the gap between how we acted on court and how a few of us thought and spoke away from it. I still admired my parents for what they'd done, but the life they had in mind for me was so staid, so utterly predictable. I'd also made a couple of new friends at school whose parents seemed to be loaded. That made me wonder about the possibilities. I was still unworldly, I'd be the first to admit that, but I was up for adventure.

Ashley was, by far, the sexiest boy in the squad. Tall and blond, he looked just the way I'd imagined an Ashley should. I caught him staring at my boobs one day, which now held up well against the competition. We started hanging around together. My parents seemed happy. How could two ball-kids be anything but wholesome?

Ashley's father was a bookmaker. That sounded cool and I told Ashley I loved reading. He shook his head in disbelief. When he explained, I felt myself turning crimson all over. So embarrassing! Nothing my father had ever said or done could have been dopier. Ashley saw it as a great joke. I grabbed him and made him promise he would never, ever, post anything about it. 'Sure,' he said, still smiling. I pulled him to me and kissed him sloppily on the mouth. I hadn't had much practice at that sort of thing. But I soon learnt a lot about the male member. What a weird word that is!

I spent Christmas and New Year with Ashley and his parents, Edward and Chloe, at their holiday house at Port Fairy. I liked Edward. He talked and laughed a lot, mainly at his own jokes. His favourite phrase was 'Well, we'll see about that, won't we?' It was friendly and challenging at the same time. The third day we were there, Ashley and I decided to keep score of the 'we'll see about thats'. We'd counted eleven by lunchtime but called it quits because I couldn't help giggling each time Edward used the phrase.

The view from the holiday house of the hills and the sea was awesome, a world away from our crowded duplex in Yarraville with its stale aromas of down-at-heel life.

On the way home from Port Fairy, Edward asked how we felt about being in the Australian Open for the last time as we'd be too old the following year.

'Weird,' I said, 'like happy and sad all at once.'

He looked at me in the rear-view mirror, nodded and said, 'Yeah, I can understand'. Then he added, 'If you're going to be on court for the men's final, we'll need to have a chat.'

Ashley and I looked at each other, puzzled, but said in unison, 'Sure.' I added that as it got to the end of the tournament there were fewer ball-kids needed.

Edward replied, 'Well, we'll see about that, won't we?'

It's hard to describe the excitement of being on court for the championship matches. They simply couldn't happen without us. Imagine Serena Williams having to run around and collect the balls, then test them and Velcro the chosen ones to her knickers. It'd have been a fun sight for five minutes then most of the spectators would have gone for a beer. Nadal would have been exhausted just from running back and forth for one of his towels. And some players need someone to yell at, beside themselves.

I'd talked to a one kid, Thomas, who'd been on court with Andy Murray and had to pick up Murray's racquet after he belted the ground with it. Thomas claimed he'd smuggled the broken racquet out after the game and sold it to a schoolfriend for a hundred dollars. That made me wonder. It's one thing to get a ball-kid food allowance and to be able to take your court uniform home. But I was now at the age where clothes and shoes and bling counted for a lot more than a sweat-stained Adidas sun cap hanging on my bedroom wall.

There were a few upsets in the early rounds that year. Murray was in good form and so well-behaved on court a joke went around that his new coach had changed his meds. Nadal was nearing the end of his career but was still full of that never-say-die energy that made him such an incredible player. He was fussier than ever about lining up his drink bottles, now in a precise north-south orientation which he checked with a compass after every drink.

Against some predictions, but to our great relief, it was a Nadal-Murray final. The crowd was with Nadal, the 'not-so-smart-money', as Edward called it, with Murray. It was a nail-biter, including for Edward and Ashley and Chloe in the stands, and me on the court.

The four of us, however, were chewing for reasons rather different from everyone else.

Nadal took the first set, Murray the next two, and Nadal the fourth. It was locked at four games all in the fifth and final set, with Murray to serve. It was time for us to act. There was a big problem, though. I was at the wrong end of the court – Nadal's. But I'd left my world of innocence far behind and was nothing if not resolute.

*

With time on my hands, these days I occasionally watch a replay of the match. Unlike all the so-called experts, I know exactly what to look for. It still gives me a thrill to see how well it worked.

With the score at 30–all, one of the kids at Nadal's end drops a ball. She tries to kick the ball up but only succeeds in sending it neatly along the sideline (almost as if she'd practised doing just that). Like a good ball-kid, she races after it, as both the kids assigned to the net are on the other, umpire's, side. She catches the ball just past the net and, as she's been trained to do, speeds to the nearest end of the court, Murray's. He serves. It's an ace, 40–30. (Crunch time.) The ball-kid now races over to Murray, holding a ball in her left hand and a towel in her right. There's a momentary look of surprise on Murray's face as he turns towards her. He hasn't signalled for a towel. Now she holds the ball out in front of her.

(Edward presses the small remote control he's carrying. He's very, very pleased with me as I've pointed the clasp on my bracelet straight at Murray's right eye. It's a few seconds before the near-invisible spray takes effect, something to do with body warmth or moisture, giving me time to return to the ball-kid spot at the back of the court.)

Suddenly, Murray drops his racquet, clutches his face and collapses to his knees in agony. The umpire hurries over. After a five-minute medical timeout, Murray, his right eye a vicious red, returns to the court to massive applause. It's not enough, and who can blame him? He loses the set 4–6, and the championship.

That made Edward an extremely wealthy man. He'd taken a huge risk in placing the bet, especially as he couldn't arrange everything – he just hated to use the word 'fix'. I was proud beyond words of my role but had to be exceedingly careful not to show it. I burst into tears as soon as the match finished and kept blubbering an apology for my stupid mistake with the wayward ball, even as the presentation ceremony was getting under way. I whimpered that I'd been so unprofessional.

That word went over well. Everyone comforted me, they were so sweet

The atmosphere at the ceremony was understandably muted, Nadal gracious in victory, Murray stunned in defeat. Naturally, there followed excited speculation about what had happened. The consensus was that something nasty must have brushed Murray's eye. That was certainly true, though not in the way everyone imagined. As a precaution, and to be seen to be doing something I suppose, flustered tennis officials rounded up all the towels, Nadal's included, and sent them away for chemical analysis.

Afterwards, we went out for dinner, Ashley and his parents, me and mine. That was incredibly tricky. My parents were blissfully ignorant of the fact that their eldest child would soon be a very rich young lady, providing Edward kept his promise. I knew he would. My story could send him to gaol for a long time.

My performance at dinner was brilliant, if I do say so myself. Not sullen, just very quiet, clearly upset by what had happened to poor Andy.

'Do you think I should send him a get-well card?' I asked, my voice trembling.

'That's a lovely thought, Sam,' my mother said. She always called me that, rather than Samantha, when she was feeling affectionate. Then she looked carefully at my wrist and exclaimed, 'Why, darling, that's a new bracelet.'

'It certainly is,' Edward declared. 'My small gift to your daughter for all she's done for tennis and our two families.'

He didn't mention it was the second bracelet he given me.

*

My parents were deeply upset when I left Australia so soon afterwards. Edward used all his powers of persuasion to convince them to let me accompany him, Chloe and Ashley to Florida. Miami, he announced, 'was the tennis capital of the world'. There, he would pursue his interests in tennis administration. I was a natural fit for his small team, he argued, carefully noting the venture was likely to be very lucrative. As for the weather, it was 'just so much better than Melbourne's'.

'I just don't understand what's going on, Samantha,' my mother lamented. 'Yes, it's good that Edward thinks so highly of you, and I suppose sports management is a worthwhile occupation. But it all seems to be such a rush. Why can't you wait a year or two? Another thing,' she continued. 'I know that you and Ashley are close friends but you're far too young to be in a serious relationship. My head's in such a whirl.'

So was mine and I could sense an urgency in Edward which clearly suggested he knew something I didn't particularly want to find out.

'Mum,' I said, with as much sincerity as I could muster, 'you and Dad always wanted me to become a ball-kid. I'm truly grateful you pushed me. You helped me realise I really want to make a career out of tennis. I'm not good enough to be a top player, I know that. I'm certain I can contribute to the game, though. I've learnt so much from Edward. And it does pay well.'

My parents, especially my father, remained sceptical. But they agreed to a year away, a sort of internship as they described it to their friends. One year became two, by which I was legally an adult. Me time.

I still miss Australia, though I've had a life most others could only dream about. My parents eventually came round. Now they readily concede they never imagined such an existence, travelling the world and visiting Ashley and me and their two grandchildren every year. They're chuffed that there's now a scholarship for ball-kids from underprivileged backgrounds, funded anonymously but bearing their name.

'Who would have thought there'd be so much money in tennis balls,' my father joked one day when I was farewelling them at the airport. Then he did something that unnerved me. He winked.

'Oh, don't be such a tease,' my mother chided. 'Just be thankful we produced such a wonderful daughter.'

I don't see as much of Edward and Chloe now that they've moved to Monaco. These days Edward describes himself as semi-retired. Maybe. Whenever there's a big upset in a major tennis tournament, Ashley and I smile at each other and silently mouth the phrase, 'Well, we'll see about retirement, won't we?'

A tongue lashing

You're not going to enjoy this, but it's time for home truths. Our life together must change, which means you must change. Bluntly put, you've become extremely boring to live with. What happened to the fun-loving person that once was you?

You're always making lists, so here's the story of our tedious existence under four headings: words; food; drink; sex.

Yes, I know your friends are impressed with your vocabulary. Precipitation rather than rain, axiomatic rather than bloody obvious. But your sentences are also stuffed with phrases such as, oh really? but surely!, is that so? no kidding! They insult both our abilities.

Look at what we eat, even at restaurants. I know vegetarianism is all the go. But tell me this, just how many brown rice and nut meat casseroles with a side order of tofu chips are you planning to eat in your lifetime? I want variety, and a good rump steak once a week.

At least you're not teetotal, even if you do hide the bottle in the bedroom, well away from your mother's prying eyes. But Marsala? There's a lot of fine wine around. A good red might help us bond.

As for sex, you ponder why it happens so rarely. Simple answer: oral hygiene. Sucking your teeth is no substitute for cleaning them. It makes me want to puke.

Now you're getting stroppy. I can feel your blood pressure rising. How dare I berate you, you're thinking.

Well, as your tongue, I have a right to express my opinions. Change your lifestyle, or else. Here are the options – the odorous, the ulcerous, the cancerous. Perhaps all three.

Not pretty, I know, but desperate times breed desperate measures. Work with me, for both our sakes.

You've been warned.

Your call cannot be connected

Her words had comforted us like none other. 'It's an illness, you can't be blamed,' she'd soothe as a newcomer to the group blubbered his or her way through a confession

We all knew the humiliation of declaring to a roomful of strangers that our lives were out of control. How most of the time we just sat there, glassy-eyed, obsessed with the next surreptitious glance.

At least we'd accepted the need for treatment. She seemed the perfect guide, an ex-addict herself, understanding but tough. Two people who brought prohibited items to a meeting spent days in the Box.

'Let that be a lesson to you all,' she warned.

Then, just as our first session for the new term got under way, a red iPhone slipped from her carry bag, clattering to the floor. She turned a shocking, deathly colour.

Sleek and shiny – my hands tremble as I write these words – the iPhone looked so beautiful lying there. I felt such desire to pick it up, to caress its glistening surfaces, to listen to its chirrups of satisfaction at knowing how much we cherished it.

But I'd responded well to treatment. I slapped my face so hard my eyes watered. That snapped the others out of their trance.

'Come on,' I urged, my voice wavering, 'we know what we have to do.'

'I'm sorry, I'm sorry, I'm sorry,' she whimpered, her eyes begging for a reprieve.

We felt no malice, just profound sadness and disappointment. Gently we took her by the arms, opened the Box, and strapped her in. The door locked automatically. It would reopen only when she, like others before her, had been reprogrammed.

The iPhone still lay on the floor. I could feel its evil pull. Two people in the group excused themselves and rushed to the bathroom. I heard them crying and throwing up.

My breathing shallowed. No, I pleaded with myself, you must not relapse, the group needs you. I took the emergency kit off the wall, put on the special gloves, and picked up the iPhone. Even through the thick material, I could feel it nuzzling my hands, craving affection.

Tears streaming down her face, one of the others switched on the Pulverizer. The machine whirred, the iPhone vanished amid a terrible crunching sound. As I slumped to the floor, I thought I heard a phone ringing, then another one, and another.

Lost for words

I'm in trouble, big fucking trouble. Slipped in the shower, broke the glass screen. Cut my leg badly. Blood everywhere. I need one word, just one. Someone's bound to hear, these apartments have thin walls.

But I cannot make a sound, not even a single grunt. I stare at the chip in the back of my hand. Expired, Expired, Expired, it flashes. Where have my words gone? I can't have used them all up. Maybe I've been hacked. Bastards.

And to think this is my own doing, my naive, egotistic attempt to make a fairer world. We knew distributing wealth was a gimmick, distributing power a fraud. At least we could all start with the same number of words. One billion to last a lifetime. A generous allocation, democracy in action.

I bathed in the acclaim, received the highest honours. Gave interviews and speeches. Could I have used up all my ration that way? No, I've never been a gabbler. I swear a lot, but not enough for this.

Can only have been those doctors. The ones we sent to gaol. Stealing chips from the dead, particularly the young. Road accidents a blessing, ambulance drivers on the take. The word-chip mafia the judge had called them.

I get it now, but all too late. I was in hospital not long after they were sentenced, infected toe, that must have been when the switch took place. A sympathiser, inside job.

I should try to leave a note, but I can only sit here, leaking red, feeling most unwell. Mustn't panic, though. Mustn't. Only speeds up the heart rate, blood flow, blood loss. If only we'd fitted the device with an alarm. But I was adamant. I knew best. Nothing would ever go wrong.

Nothing. Ever.

Dr Watson wrestles with his work-life balance

John Watson sat in his hotel room in Bali, pondering the email he'd just written. It didn't say much. Only that he was enjoying his holiday and grateful for his travel agent's help. Yet, for Watson, the message was a window into his heart, 'Dear Annalise' a declaration, not a salutation. He'd even included 'When you travel again, where would you like to go?' Rereading that sentence, he decided it carried an awkward hint of possible time together. Watson deleted it. A tug of war followed. Restore. Delete. Restore. Delete. Finally, Watson persuaded himself the sentence was sufficiently ambiguous to survive.

The sign-off took another twenty minutes. 'Yours sincerely' or 'Yours truly' sounded archaic, even by Watson's own standards. 'Regards,' whether of the 'warm' or 'best' variety, were so commonplace. Eventually, after much soul-searching and several gulps of Johnny Walker Blue Label, he settled for 'Affectionately, John Watson'. He wondered if he should add, MD but refrained. He took another sip and clicked Send.

He'd done it!

It was the first even vaguely romantic message Watson had written in years. Given the stress it caused him, he understood why. Was he being foolish? Would he feel the same way if he'd actually met Annalise, rather than just talking to her on the phone?

He stood, stretched, poured himself another drink and went out to the balcony. Beyond the modest hotel on the outskirts of Ubud, the rice fields lay quiet, blushed by a faint moon. He stared into the night, a curious mix of contentment and restlessness upon him.

*

Watson was deeply unconscious when his mobile trilled. As his mind slowly defogged, its first thought was that Annalise was calling. That, of course, was absurd. Watson reached for his official tone.

'Watson speaking.'

'Good evening, sir,' came a fruity, enthusiastic voice. 'Inspector Ivan Inkling, sir, Scotland Yard Special Investigations, sir. Hope I haven't disturbed you, sir, but looking into a matter sir, on which you may be able to assist. Sir.'

'I'll certainly help if I can,' Watson said, puzzled by the buzz of sirs.

'We understand, sir, you are an acquaintance of a Mr Sherlock Holmes, a man well known to the Yard and, I should add, sir, highly respected.'

'Yes, off course, inspector, I know Mr Holmes well. Tell me what this is about.'

'Well, sir, very regrettable matter. Mr Holmes has been attacked and beaten up rather badly, sir. In a London hospital he is, sir, fractured left arm and severe bruising. Took a rather nasty blow to the head too, sir.'

'Why that's terrible news,' Watson said, catching himself just as he was about to add 'sir'. 'Thank you for letting me know, inspector. Is there any way in which I can help?'

'Well, glad you asked that question, sir,' Inkling said. His tone became deliberate. 'The thing is, Dr Watson, sir, we understand that you and Mr Holmes have had something of a falling out of late. Been a bit written and broadcast about it, sir, as you may be aware. Even on the BBC,' the inspector added, as if that clinched whatever point he was trying to make. There was a pause before he went on, 'We thought you might be able to shed some light on the assault, sir.'

'Well, I can't, inspector, and I'm surprised you felt I could.' Watson did not hide his irritation. 'If you'd done your homework, inspector, you'd know this so-called falling out is an absurd fabrication. I simply commented in one interview that Mr Holmes was regularly credited with solving crimes that required dedicated teamwork. Often involving, I might add, the men and women of Scotland Yard.'

'Quite so, sir,' said Inkling, 'quite so. We in the Yard are only too familiar with fake news. Everywhere these days it is, sir, and a shocking thing too.' Inkling picked his way carefully through the next words. 'I should mention, sir, that we are recording this conversation. Felt it would be prudent to have you on the record.' He paused. 'Sir.'

'Are you suggesting I'm a suspect?' Watson was incredulous.

'Nothing of the sort, sir, nothing of the sort. Just that, as you know from your own occasional work as an understudy to Mr Holmes, it's important to have a precise account, sir, of who said what.'

Watson's voice simmered angrily. 'Inspector Inkling, you phone me out of the blue and in effect accuse me of involvement in a vicious attack on Mr Holmes. This is –'

'How did you know it was vicious?' the inspector cut in triumphantly. 'That is not a term I used, sir, though I readily acknowledge it is a fitting description of the nature of the assault upon our friend and mentor. It suggests to me the possibility of prior knowledge. Sir,' he added heavily.

'That is nonsensical, inspector,' Watson flared. 'I demand to know the name of your superior officer. I also suggest you get on with the business of catching the person or persons responsible for this outrage rather than making absurd phone calls in the middle of the night!'

'Actually, sir, it's just gone six p.m. here. But no matter. Interesting you raise the possibility, sir, of perhaps more than one person being involved. We'll look into it, sir, I promise you that. As for the name of my superior officer, sir, the Yard's flatter management structure means we no longer employ such terminology, sir. But you can see the full organisational chart at www.scotyard.gov.uk. That's all lower case by the way, sir. I thank you for your time, sir, we'll be in touch if we need anything further. Goodnight, or rather good morning. Sir.'

The line went dead. The bottle trembled as Watson refilled his glass.

*

Two days later, Watson's flight landed at Heathrow. He'd agonised about whether he should return early. Would Inkling see it as a sign of guilt? Watson had contacted Annalise, asking that she change his travel booking. Their email exchanges had been straightforward, though Watson noted that in Annalise's third email the 'kind regards' of the first two had become 'warmest wishes'. Encouraged by these words, he felt ready for whatever lay ahead.

He phoned Annalise from his Holland Park townhouse. But it seemed a waste to leave his carefully rehearsed words on her voicemail.

Inspector Inkling answered on the second ring. 'Welcome back, Dr Watson. What have you got for us, sir?'

'What do you mean?' Watson asked.

'Well, just thought, sir, that with you cutting your holiday short, something might have,' he paused, 'clarified.' He let that word hang in the air then added, 'Our door is open for you sir, day or night, 24/7 as our younger officers like to say.'

'If I hear anything, inspector,' Watson exhaled, 'I'll let you know.'

He put the phone down, not sure why he'd called Inkling in the first place. He sat for a long while at the kitchen bench, his mind wandering. Then suddenly he was bolt upright, dazzled not just by the sunlight now flooding the room but the brilliance of his deduction. An hour or two in his library left no doubt. He phoned Inkling, asking to see him urgently. The inspector's response made clear he was expecting a confession.

'Do you mean to say, sir,' Inkling said, staring across his desk, 'you're sure who the main suspect is but that he's dead? Ridiculous, if you ask me. Sir,' he added reluctantly.

'Do you read much, inspector?' Watson asked calmly.

'Quite frankly, I don't see what that's got to do with anything,' Inkling retorted, 'and, as I'm sure you'll appreciate, sir, what time I do have for reading is devoted to official matters.'

Watson pressed on. 'But you are familiar with the Sherlock Holmes stories and their author, Sir Arthur Conan Doyle?'

'What sort of a question is that?' Inkling snapped, so irritated that the flow of sirs now choked.

'You do realise that Doyle came to detest Holmes?'

'Well, that just doesn't add up,' Inkling said crankily. 'And where exactly is all this going? Seems to me, Dr Watson, you might have consumed one mushroom too many in Bali.'

Watson was unflustered. 'I have a simple request, inspector. I understand there's CCTV footage of the assault. Could we watch it together?'

Grudgingly, Inkling agreed.

Sherlock's image was clear but the shorter person wearing a hoodie who suddenly appeared from a doorway and lunged at Holmes, striking him hard across the head, could have been any small man with a blunt instrument.

'I'd know that figure anywhere,' Watson said, triumph and relief in his voice.

'You must be joking,' Inkling snapped.

'You should read more widely, inspector. It's Lenny Hand.'

'Lenny who?' Inkling demanded.

'A small-time crook who lurked around many Sherlock Holmes stories. Always does a little figure eight with the cosh before striking his victim. Have another look.'

Inkling replayed the footage. 'I see,' he said, his tone churlish. He reached for his mobile.

Lenny was not hard to locate. Wearing a police bracelet, he was out on bail after breaking into a house, drinking a bottle of sweet sherry and falling asleep on a couch. With the offer of a deal dangled in front of him, Lenny readily confessed he'd been hired by Professor James Moriarty, Holmes's arch-enemy.

Moriarty was already in gaol for people smuggling, an area of criminal activity he boasted to his associates was entirely in keeping with the business model Conan Doyle had envisaged for him. Not used to being called sir by anyone, he quickly succumbed to Inkling's interrogation style.

'All right, I'll say it one more time,' Moriarty pleaded, 'just stop being so polite to me. I was asked by Jimmy Doyle, Conan Doyle's great grandson, to find a hit person for the job.'

Jimmy Doyle was short, round-faced and well spoken. He'd hardly entered the interview room when he declared, 'Inspector, there's really no need to waste time on all that, You know why you're here, et cetera et cetera palaver. Great grandfather would be very proud of me. I've preserved the family honour, nothing more, nothing less.'

Jimmy reached into his coat and extracted a single sheet of paper which he unfolded. 'All male descendants of Sir Arthur receive a copy of this directive on their twenty-first birthday. I would like to read it into my statement.'

Inkling looked at his colleagues and shrugged. Jimmy read aloud, 'Sherlock Holmes, my most famous character, forgot his great debt to me. I am not talking about money, Heaven forbid! I am talking about the principle of literary figures assuming a life of their own, as if their authors were mere intermediaries. Holmes claimed to be the father of modern policing. An utter falsehood. It was me, I, one's very own self, Sir Arthur Conan Doyle, who can rightfully claim paternity.'

Jimmy paused, then read with slow, precise emphasis, 'I hereby direct my male heirs to keep a close eye on Holmes. If they judge him to be getting above his station, they should take whatever action deemed necessary to remind him of his place.

Jimmy pushed the document towards Inkling. 'That's all I need say, inspector,' he concluded cheerily. 'Guilty as charged, whatever that is, and glad to be so.'

'But why now?' asked Inkling, 'I don't understand.'

'Simple, inspector, simple,' Jimmy responded. 'Do you know there are two new Sherlock Holmes films in the making, plus three more television series, plus any number of board games featuring Holmes the hero, plus parks and avenues all over the globe being named in his honour. Almost daily it seems. Just imagine how that makes the Doyle family feel. We've all got our breaking point, inspector.'

Inkling nodded thoughtfully. He stared at Watson. 'How did you know?' he asked.

'Elementary, my dear inspector,' Watson replied, 'it pays to be well read, to truly understand character.'

Inkling shook his head in admiration. He even managed a smile. 'Well done. Sir.'

*

Watson should have been relieved by this whirl of events. Inkling's flow of 'sirs' had been restored with the force of a fire hose. Watson had visited Sherlock in hospital. His battered appearance was a shock but their conversation gave Watson hope for the future.

'I'm very proud of you, John,' Sherlock said. 'You're up there with the best of us.'

'I learned from the best,' Watson replied, surprised by this mutual display of magnanimity.

'I am sorry there's been some tension between us,' Sherlock continued. 'I know I've never been the easiest of characters. Seems these days there's actually a profession called relationship counselling. Imagine that. I wonder if it might help us – you and me, that is? Just a suggestion. What do you think?'

Watson was taken aback. The idea of Sherlock asking for his opinion was so novel he wondered about his companion's mental state. He quietly reprimanded himself. 'An excellent idea,' he said, smiling warmly at Sherlock, 'I'll look into it right away.'

*

If Watson could start afresh with Sherlock, could he not do the same with Annalise? He sat in his study, gazing at the half-written email on the screen. What could he say that would rekindle whatever had been kindling? The day after his return from Bali, Annalise had sent a message inviting him to dinner. Dinner! The image of the two of them sitting in a halo of candlelight elated and flustered him in equal measure. Even as he wrote his response, thanking Annalise but regretting his pre-occupation with an important case, he knew it was all wrong.

This time, it would be different.

Dear Annalise

I fear that earlier I may have appeared ungracious in responding to your kind invitation to dinner. I hope I will be granted a second chance.

I would be delighted to be your companion. I consider we have much of mutual interest to discuss and would like to test that hypothesis at a date and time convenient to you.

I have no food allergies.

In case you are not already aware, I take the liberty of noting that I am a fully trained physician. Ill-health is the last thing I would wish upon anyone, most especially you. But if there is anything of a medical nature, anything at all that troubles you, I stand ready to assist. It would be a pleasure to offer my advice and services, free of any charge or obligation.

Yours as ever

John Watson MD

Self-satisfied, Watson mused that the final paragraph played to his strengths. That was a cliché of course, he knew that. But then so much about love seemed to be exactly that. He thought about crossing his fingers as the message flew on its way. Silly superstition, he chided himself. He took a deep breath, a large slug of Blue Label and, with his toes crossed as much as his slippers would allow, clicked Send.

Bathurst for beginners

It wasn't nearly as bad being inside as I'd imagined. My family was a bit embarrassed of course but most of them still showed up in court to wave me goodbye. I'm the first of us ever to get my name in the paper and they wanted to share the moment. I can see them down the years saying proudly, 'Seems like only yesterday that Johnno did time. Got the clipping here somewhere. Want to see it?'

Even now, I feel strongly about the exercise routine. Makes no sense to me why they lock people up and then worry about keeping them fit. Better off letting them go to seed. I mean, how many fat people escape from gaol? It's the fit, skinny ones that make a break for it. Lesson there, surely. Cut out the exercise and keep the prisoners podgy.

Got to give credit where credit's due, though. Bathurst changed my life. Bit of time on my hands for once. Guess that's how the idea popped into my head. What's missing in our prison system, I asked myself? Guidebooks, that's what. New arrivals every day and each of them has to start from scratch. Ridiculous! Why not something like *Behind Goulburn's Gates* or *Perusing Port Philip* to help them settle in.

I put the idea to a few of the lads. Took to it at once they did. And not just the inmates. Prison governor volunteered himself as patron of our editorial committee. Bit wary at first we were, but soon saw that his support could come in real handy. After all, we wanted to include things like a detailed plan of the prison, great and not so great escapes, and a top ten of the best and worst warders. Other officials might have been a bit suspicious. Not our governor.

'Boys,' he said one day, 'this is the biggest breakthrough in the nation's gaols since the end of transportation.'

'What do mean, sir?' one committee member asked, a worried look on his face. 'Aren't the buses runnin' any more? How'll my mum get here to see me?'

The governor gave him a kindly look.

The first print run of *Bathurst for Beginners* sold out within ten days. Everyone, it seemed, knew someone who was about to go in or looked a sure bet in the future. The official launch at Dymocks, by none other than the Premier, attracted huge TV coverage, no doubt helped by the fact that the three members of the editorial committee in attendance, including yours truly I'm proud to say, were in leg-irons and handcuffs. A reasonable precaution. After all, one of us had contributed an article entitled 'My First 20 Years'. Not the most lucid piece in the book but he'd promised to do a better job at the thirty-year mark.

We waited nervously for the reviews. To our great relief, Eddie Obeid gave it a big wrap. It was, he wrote, 'a sensitive and insightful account of the needs and fears of those about to open a new chapter in their lives'. Some of the boys had a bit of difficulty working out what that meant. I told them that Eddie was saying that our little volume would help you stay in one piece in the clink.

The Woman's Weekly gave us a glowing report. It especially liked the section 'Tried and Tested Prison Recipes'. 'Every Australian', it wrote, 'is indebted to those who've taken the time and trouble to work out what actually goes into that cheap, nutritious fare.'

From then on, we never looked back. So if at any time, anywhere, you find yourself on the wrong side of the law, there'll be a guide to the local lock-up produced by our little company. You'll find a listing of all the titles on Amazon. As long as you've got at least three days bail and a credit card that works, they guarantee delivery before your time starts.

We've done well financially but it's taken a toll. Travelling the world, searching for talent with the right sort of inside knowledge, hasn't been easy. Nowadays, I limit myself to Australia. Even here, though, what with the updates and the new editions, it's like painting the Harbour Bridge. I'm in and out of the nation's gaols like a blooming jack-in-the-box.

Still, I shouldn't complain. I had an idea and I saw it through. And to think it all started with a bunch of unpaid parking fines.

Muesli bars for Dad

Hanson was dead. That, at least, was good news. Trouble was, I'd been paid to kill him and someone else had beaten me to it. I stood there, the big question hammering at my brain. How would I tell Dad? After all, he'd promised to forget about the twenty thou I owed him if I took care of Hanson.

What could I do? I hadn't committed a single crime. Not even a break and entry, as the front door had been wide open. Then my mobile rang. I fumbled for it thinking, shit, hadn't I turned the bloody thing off? For a fleeting moment, I had an image of arriving outside Hanson's study, gun in hand, my phone ringing, me answering, and a very much alive Reginald Hanson at the other end asking what the hell I was up to.

But, of course, it wasn't Hanson. It was Dad.

'Well?' When he used that word, it was always a question.

'Everything's okay,' I said, which was true after a fashion.

'No trouble?' Dad's questions were also very economical.

'Nup,' which, again, was sort of true.

'Well, you better come on back then. Guess that settles the debt.'

Dad was in an unusually good mood when I arrived home. He would have been in an even better one if he'd known that not only was his enemy dead but that I still owed him.

'Better have a celebratory drink,' he said. He levered himself out of the expensive leather chair he'd treated himself to after a very good trading year, as he put it, and retrieved the Johnny Walker Green Label and two heavy crystal glasses. 'A toast to our late colleague,' he drawled.

That seemed an unusual way of describing Hanson. He was certainly late but he'd never been much of a colleague.

'Sure,' I said. I was nervous.

'No trouble then?' Dad's questions were often also statements.

'No, all very smooth.'

'What did the prick have to say for himself before you plugged him?'

'Nothing, not a peep.' I was getting very jittery now.

'Just like all blowhards,' Dad said with a grin. 'Point the business end of a gun at them and they turn to bloody water. Cheers!'

'Cheers,' I returned, trying to sound, well, cheerful.

Dad looked at me quizzically. 'What's up, Simon?' he asked. 'You sound a bit down in the dumps for a bloke who's just cleared his debts. Yeah, your first killing always feels a bit strange. But you'll adjust pretty quickly. I speak from experience, you know.'

'Yes, Dad,' was all I could say. 'Sorry, I've got to go, I'm meeting Vicky.'

'Aw,' he seemed a bit disappointed. 'Righto, then, well, have a good time and,' he paused, 'well done. I'm proud of you!'

*

'But why tell him?' Vicky asked. 'Hanson's dead, your father's happy, you don't have to pay him back. Why can't you just let it be?'

'Well, it's simply wrong, that's why. It's like taking money under false pretences.'

'Come on, Simon!' Vicky said with exasperation. 'You were quite happy to go off and kill another man. Now you're talking about right and wrong. It's bizarre.'

'But that's just the point,' I said, 'I had a contractual arrangement and I failed to honour it –'

'Contractual arrangement, indeed,' Vicky cut in. 'You're starting to sound like a lawyer. It's hardly your fault you didn't kill someone. Your intentions were honest. Let's drop it and talk about something else. Name the subject.'

'Breasts,' I said softly, after a brief pause.

'Breasts? Breasts!' Vicky raised her voice so sharply that a few of the other drinkers turned and stared at us.

'Yes, breasts,' I said, quietly and deliberately. 'It's the only subject that can distract me, that will give me comfort. Tell me what you think of them.'

'You've just botched a murder and you want to talk about boobs!' Vicky's tone was incredulous but at least she'd lowered her voice.

'I didn't botch it, that's not fair,' I said defensively. 'I just need something that'll take my mind of my dilemma.'

'Dilemma? Really Simon, there'll be other opportunities to shoot someone. Don't be so melodramatic.'

I sat there in silence, looking at my drink. After a minute or two, Vicky smiled, reached across and took my hand. 'Okay,' she said, shaking her head, 'if it's the only thing that'll make you feel better, tits it is.'

*

I came down late next morning. Dad was still at the table, the smeared remnants of bacon and egg on the plate in front of him. The smell of charred toast hung on the air. He was chewing a muesli bar as he read the newspaper.

'Well, well,' he said, with a grin. 'Big night?'

'Sort of,' I replied. I found a bowl, half filled it with cornflakes, drowned them in milk and sat down.

'Got a few things I need to sort out this morning,' Dad said, 'but waited for you, wanted to read you this.' He held up the *Daily Truth*. 'Hanson made page one. The best part is this. "In what police describe as a professional hit, Reginald Hanson, well known criminal identity, was shot dead in his home yesterday afternoon." Mmm, professional hit,' Dad mused. 'I'm chuffed by those words, son. Your mother would have been too. Pity she's no longer with us.' He glanced at the photo on the sideboard. 'Pity,' he repeated, a rare softness in his gravelly voice.

There was momentary silence, then Dad spoke again. 'Only thing I find a bit odd is that police forensics are quoted as saying the killer used a .32. I thought you carried a .38?'

My heart was suddenly beating like a drum. I said as calmly as I could, 'You're good, Dad, very quick. I changed guns, just in case. If the police start snooping, they'll find I'm the lawful registered owner of a .38. The other one's kept well out of sight.'

'Apart from special outings, like visiting Reggie boy,' Dad smiled. 'Good thinking, son. You've got the makings of a top-flight crim.'

*

'He's on to me, for sure,' I said to Vicky that night.

'Nonsense,' she replied. 'He's just observant. That's how you stay at the top. Sounds to me like you handled it pretty well.'

That night, I slept restlessly. It was partly Vicky's flat. Once it warmed up in the summer, it stayed that way, day and night. But it was more than just the clammy atmosphere, it was the dream.

I was in court, charged with Hanson's murder.

The prosecutor, a smartly dressed woman whose name was Harriet Thompson, was questioning me, taunting me really, about the statement I'd given to the police. 'Mr Peters, you really expect this court to believe that you told your father you'd killed Reginald Hanson but you hadn't because someone else had already shot him. You didn't tell your father that because he would have been disappointed and it would have not cleared your debt. You tell your father one thing and the police and the court something entirely different. Is that about the sum of it?'

'Yes,' I replied meekly.

'And just which version of events do you expect us to accept?'

'Well, the truth is, I didn't kill Hanson.'

'Were you disappointed at your failure to carry out a criminal act?'

'Objection, Your Honour,' said my lawyer from Legal Aid. Dad had refused to help me unless I pleaded guilty.

'On what grounds?' the judge asked.

'Um, the defendant's feelings are not relevant.'

'Oh yes, they are,' the judge declared, signalling to everyone where he thought the case was going. 'Dismissed.'

'Well, Mr Peters. Were you disappointed?'

'Yes.'

'You were quite happy at the thought of committing murder?'

'Well, um, I –'

'A simple yes or no will suffice, Mr Peters.'

'Yes.'

'Do you feel a failure as a killer?'

My lawyer, a small red-bearded man whose name I couldn't remember, looked as though he was about to intervene again, then gave a shrug and said nothing.

'Yes.'

'And that essentially is your defence? You'd like to have been a murderer but you blew it?'

'Well, I wouldn't put it quite that way.'

'Yes or no, Mr Peters?'

'Yes.'

I woke, perspiring, drained. My first thought was that I needed to kill someone. I was clearly going to go mad if I didn't. Then the idea hit me. I shook Vicky awake.

'Oh God, what's the time?' she groaned.

'Just on five.'

'Simon, what on earth's going on?'

'Sorry, I just had to tell you. I know how to sort it out.'

'Sort what out? What do you mean? Aw, no,' she groaned again, 'you're still obsessing about Hanson.'

I told her what I planned to do.

She looked at me, bleary-eyed, and said, 'You're mad. Starkers. Now let me get back to sleep!'

I felt miffed she hadn't been more receptive. But Vicky was never much of a morning person.

*

'You're sure you want to handle it this way?' asked the grey-looking thin man across the desk. Martin Burroughs had unusually fat lips, as if they'd been botoxed. It gave him a strange, ugly look. He'd stand out in a crowd. I doubted that was an asset in a private detective.

'There's a risk you'll draw attention to yourself,' he said. 'Not that I'd mention it to the police. No risk of that, even if I am an ex-copper. But you know how these things work, Mr Simons. Word gets around. A bit of buzz about a bloke who's looking for the bloke who killed the bloke the first bloke was supposed to. Get my drift?'

'Peters,' I corrected.

He looked at me, puzzled. 'Oh, yeah, yeah,' he said after a moment or two. 'Got it, yeah, sorry. Anyway, you see what I'm getting at?'

'I do,' I said, 'and I want to go ahead.'

'Okay, your call,' he responded with a shake of the head.

'How long do you think it'll be before we know something?' I asked.

'How long's a piece of string, Mr Simons, aw sorry, Peters? But I promise you this: you'll know something the moment I do.'

*

Burroughs was as good as his word. But not as good as the real police. Half an hour before he phoned me, to 'report developments' in his dull ex-copper's voice, I had a call from Dad.

'For once in their lives, the bloody cops have worked it out,' he said, matter-of-factly.

'What are you talking about?'

'I think you might have done your dough on that Burroughs bloke. Don't worry about how I know, I just do. When you get a chance, could you bring me some clean clothes and muesli bars. The ones without dried fruit, remember. You know how much it disagrees with me.'

'Have you lost your marbles?'

'It'll be on the news pretty soon.'

It was. Dad had been arrested for conspiring to murder Reginald Hanson. Turned out he'd contracted a well-known hitman to do the job.

To this day, it's hard for me to truly convey the anger I felt, the sense of betrayal. Imagine your own father going behind your back like that, having such little faith in you.

Naturally enough, in the lead-up to his trial, the police called me in for questioning.

'We notice you haven't been visiting your father in gaol,' one of them said. 'Given that you live with him, at least most of the time, that seems a bit odd.'

'I'm appalled by the way he behaved,' I replied.

'I can understand that,' the other cop said, 'but your father's actions can hardly have come as a surprise. He's long had what you might describe as a strained relationship with making an honest living.'

'I didn't see all that much of him until recently, after my mother died,' I said. 'I don't stick my nose in his business and he keeps his out of mine.'

'Which is?' the same cop asked.

'I'm a swimming instructor.'

'I can see you're pretty fit,' he said, nodding. 'But what about that twenty grand that went from one of his accounts into yours?'

If he thought that would startle me, he was wrong.

'Nothing mysterious,' I shrugged. 'He was helping me buy a car.'

'But you're still driving that old Mazda.'

'I'm still looking at the possibilities. Don't get much for twenty thousand these days.'

The two cops nodded in agreement. They asked a few more inane questions, gave me some advice about second-hand cars, then glanced at each other.

'What do you reckon?' one asked.

'Waste of bloody time,' the other replied.

'Go on, piss off,' they said in unison.

*

Unlike Dad, I can't really hang on to a grudge. So after he was gaoled for sixteen years, I drove to Goulburn to see him, clean clothes and muesli bars in hand.

Dad started to apologise but I cut him off. 'You let me down, Dad, you really did. I thought you trusted me, that you had faith in me. You shamed me. Nothing can ever make up for that. You're a liar and a double-dealer. That's the reality.'

'Now hang on, son,' he replied, sounding hurt. 'Double-dealer I might be. But liar? Seems that both of us might have twisted the truth. So it's all square on that charge. Okay, I should have trusted you to do the job. I just didn't want to take any chances. You need to understand, son, that's how parents are. I'm sorry, I really am. You kept your end of the bargain, or tried to, even if you did tell a few porkies along the way. Why don't we call it quits? No point in you festering away on the outside and me festering away in here, is there?'

I sat there for a few minutes, chewing my lip. Finally, what could I say but, 'No, Dad.'

'That's the spirit,' he said brightly. 'By the way, keep the money if you haven't already spent it. You can also have my Merc, long as you promise to look after it and the cops don't nab it. And take Vicky on a holiday, Sicily maybe. I can give you some contacts there. Never know, you might pick up a few tips from the pros. After that,' he continued, sounding like someone issuing instructions before heading off on holiday, 'if there's anything left in the kitty, I can never have too many muesli bars. But don't forget, no dried fruit. Gives me terrible gas!'

'You don't have to tell me that, Dad,' I said, shaking my head. 'I wouldn't do it to the other inmates.'

He chuckled and patted me on the back. 'At heart, you're a good lad,' he said with a wink.

Going bush

Helen had never anticipated how much difference there could be between being a visitor, which she had been with increasing frequency, and being a local. As a visitor, you could relax precisely because you knew home was over the horizon. Now it was a boundary, not a promise of freedom.

She tried not to judge but wondered how those with a view so limitless took in so little. Perhaps city people were just the same. Perhaps they too had no interest in what went on beyond the immediate neighbourhood. But this was better disguised in the city, where people were bombarded by the outside world whether they liked it or not. They might choose not to take notice, but they could hardly avoid it entirely. Here, you could get by on local knowledge alone. There was a sense of disconnection she had never imagined possible.

How was it that the bush that stretched for miles, with its seamless mix of browns and greyish greens and blues and hints of red, could be so still and silent and yet leave her ears ringing? She wrote to Amanda about a cacophony of silence. She found the sense of being confined hard to distil and played around with it in her head before writing to Amanda, who was instructed to pass on the letter to other friends.

Have you ever felt you're living under a dome, like one of those clear plastic covers you see in cake shops? What's weird is that I have this sense both of infinity and of being hemmed in. I can't see all that much from the back of the house except the little bump of the ridge. But from the front of the house, the view stretches for miles, finally ending in that amazing line of the horizon.

Then if you look up, you sense the sky never-ending, of going on forever. At night, it's truly amazing. The stars crackle; they seem to be alive, fizzing and popping even though they're still pretty tiny and you know they're millions of miles away. They're not as energetic if there's a moon but you still see them in a way that never happens in the city. And when there is a moon, particularly if it's full or close to full, it's completely different to watching it at home (oops, this is home, but you know what I mean, Lindfield, Mum's place). In the city, the moon seems to trail indifferently across the sky. It leaves a sort of incidental light on the land. I guess there's really too much competition for it to do anything else. Here, the moon seems to rise across the land; you watch it on the land, not the sky. It's the land that gives it definition and subtlety and almost an aroma.

You remember when we did that cruise together not long after Philip died and Mum decided that what I needed, besides a new life, was a bit of sea air? There was one night, I'm sure you can recall it, when there was a full moon. And someone remarked that you didn't really watch it in the sky, you watched it on the sea. It's the same here. We're marooned in this little house on an ocean of bush, which swells and rises and flattens in the moonlight. I'm not certain whether I'm watching the moonlight through the land or the other way around.

Anyway, where was I? I started talking about cake covers. What I'm really getting at is that, despite this sense of space and the thrill of moonlight, I still feel hemmed in. To be quite honest, I'd never thought much about horizons before. Here, I often think of nothing else. It's as if the hills over the river really have no choice but to go upwards and turn themselves into mountains. They push and stretch themselves high enough and far enough that they merge into a single blue line, a bit like a rim at the edge of a crater. The really unsettling thing is that I feel my whole world is now inside this crater. Yet I know it isn't, or at least it shouldn't be, that beyond that line there's an extraordinary world of colour and excitement and things that were part of me and I hope still are.

I suppose what it comes down to is that when I look at the horizon I really can't imagine anything more beautiful – you know what it's like when you see something exquisite and you feel incredibly excited and humbled at the same time. But when I think about the horizon, it's as though I'm being taunted.

Are you still with me? These are not exactly the sort of things we spent much time talking about when I was in Sydney. Here, I think about them most of the time. What I find odd and discomfiting is that people around here seem to go out of their way to avoid showing what's inside them. That's not because they're stupid or anything like that (though Mum clearly thinks that dropped gees and swearing are a sure sign of mental defect!). It's as though they're scared that if they started thinking, really thinking about all this stillness and silence and space, they just wouldn't be able to cope. So they stick with footy and cricket and who's up who, and who got really pissed at the pub yesterday. They cling to the clear, definable bits and pieces of life and avoid the softnesses and unknowables. Some of them go to church of course. That seems as close as they're prepared to concede that there might be a few big questions floating around. But when you think about it, I guess you go to church to hear the answers not the questions. By the way, do you still go?

In her next letter, Helen wrote about her new neighbours, thinking it might disguise her own feelings.

I want to tell you about Angus Watson. He's a real character. A few months after I arrived here, we went over to have afternoon tea with Angus and Emma. The name of their property, by the way, is Avondale. All these English sounding names – there's a property near here called Somerset. It's covered with big boulders and gum trees just like the English countryside! I'm thinking of drawing up a list of appropriate names for local use – Sunstroke Haven, Dustbowl, or Nightmare Acres!

We were chatting away about nothing in particular. Emma had asked polite questions about how I was settling in and that sort of thing.

Then Angus turned to me and said, 'S'pose you're pretty confused.'

'Sorry?' I replied.

'Well, about how we survive here.'

'I'm really not with you.'

'You don't have to be polite. You've ended up in this little place with these odd people.'

'Well, I don't think anyone's odd, at least those I've met.'

'That's a bad sign. You have to be odd to want to live here.'

He had a half-smile when he said this, which didn't make it any easier to get what he was driving at. Then he became quite serious.

'The thing that can drive people batty in the bush is that they think they're lonely when all they are really is alone. There's a hell of a difference. If they can't work that out pretty quickly, they're done for.'

I think I was meant to respond to this but I couldn't think of anything sensible to say. Robert and Emma didn't help by saying absolutely nothing.

So, after what seemed a long time, Angus continued. 'Why would anyone be lonely in the bush? You've got everything you need, more or less. You can always find someone to have a chat to and you've got a bit of space to work out what you want to say to them. Best of both worlds, really, don't you think?'

'But it might get a bit quiet for some people.'

'Bit quiet?' Angus seemed almost incredulous. 'Now that's just the sort of comment that you hear from city people. If it's quiet, make a bit of noise, turn the radio on, drive into town. But I tell you, it'll be your noise, no one else's, just yours. Now I got nothing against the city and people who live there. But you just drown in noise. Out here, there's noise when you want it and silence when you don't. You're the boss. Trouble is when there's silence people think they're lonely. Gawd, lonely! They're just alone, what's wrong with that?'

There was something in what Angus said. Still, I don't think loneliness is just a case of mistaken identity. If you're feeling lonely, which I do sometimes, are you supposed to say to yourself, 'Oh hang on, I'm just alone, so cheer up?'

It's not that simple, is it?

House and garden

Over the years, various owners had extended the house, with doubtful council approval. As the dwelling crept outwards, it came inevitably into territorial dispute with the garden. This had begun with a row of scribbly gums planted on the western side. Carefully nurtured by an early owner, they now stood tall. The other three boundary lines were staked out with oleanders, which dutifully brought forth robust, tedious clusters of pink and white. A scattering of undistinguished bushes inside this perimeter was intended to complete the garden.

Then a new owner planted more shrubs. Somehow that became a signal for future owners and tenants to dabble. Eventually, a straggling armada of callistemon, grevillea and cotoneaster advanced towards the house.

Most homes in the district did battle with their surrounding vegetation but this contest developed an intensity all its own. It represented the fear in many country people of being overwhelmed by nature. Even so, some of the town's residents urged the garden to victory, without ever really defining what that meant. Others stuck firmly to the idea that the garden should know its place as the supplicant of the house. Such rivalry would often bubble to the surface in the town's pub, particularly after a new owner or tenant had taken up residence.

'I 'eard she's thinkin' about plantin' the place up with poplars and liquidambars,' an advocate for the garden would drop into a conversation, hoping the spectre of a root-led invasion of the house's waterworks would spread alarm among its backers.

'News to me,' a house supporter would retort. 'Talkin to 'er meself only the other day. 'Parently, windmill's been playin' up. Water supply mightn't be so limitless after all.'

The jostling continued over many years. Then backers of both house and garden were shocked by the introduction into the contest of a new and dangerous weapon – lawn.

Edward Carroll, a schoolteacher, was a tall, sinewy man with un-kempt, sandy-coloured hair and thick tortoiseshell-framed glasses. He leased the house on his arrival and pretty much kept to himself, playing cricket occasionally when the town's eleven was denuded by hangovers or seasonal demands. Without any discussion or explanation, he re-moved some of the plantings, burned the carcasses, and painstakingly worked the soil to a fine tilth.

Then, after a day of welcome, soaking rain, he sowed the seed which the town's postmistress revealed in a confidential aside to a couple of her customers. 'Arrived by registered mail from Sydney it did.'

'Carroll's plantin' a bloody lawn!' trailed around the town like a bait on a string.

Early one Saturday afternoon, when he was away for the weekend, three of the older schoolboys carried out a sortie. When Carroll re-turned home, he was puzzled to find several large divots missing from his fledgling thatch.

The boys watched with smug pride as the samples were passed around in the pub.

'Yep, bloody lawn all right,' came the identification. 'Looks like a bent, bloody tricky one to grow round 'ere I reckon. Y'd 'ave to be a bit that way yerself ta try it.'

No one said anything directly to Carroll but several of his male stu-dents, perhaps in a display of early male preening, occasionally made high-pitched imitations of a lawnmower when he walked past.

Admiration was mixed with alarm. Interfering Carroll was taming the garden, bonding it with the house, making it habitable in an entirely ordinary, entirely urban sort of way. Furtive bar conversations took place about the possibility of midnight poisoning raids. The most serious ef-fort was aborted only two days out from what had been dubbed LP-day when the label of the intended weaponry was read closely for the first time. The contents of the can turned out to be ten-eighty, widely used to control rabbits but having no known impact on plant life. The smarter heads in the poisoning party realised the potential irony of this.

'But don't ya see, if there are any rabbits lurkin' around the house they're on our side,' one observed.

'What d'ya mean?' responded one of the lesser lights.

'Well, they want to work over the lawn too. So, if we knock 'em off it's, um, a sort of friendly fire accident.'

'Yeah, but who's lightin' a fire?'

'No, I don't mean that, ya dickhead. It's like an own goal, maybe runnin' out ya battin' partner.'

'Aw, yeah. Righto.'

Under Carroll's diligent care, the lawn thrived. Then he showed a cunning so unexpected the locals felt powerless to resist. As Christmas neared, Carroll invited the school, about thirty pupils all told, to the house. They walked out late one morning and gaped in amazement at the dazzlingly green, soft, bindii-free lawn. There had never been anything like it in the district. The only term to use was Bloody Luscious. When the children returned home that day, most of them, to their parents' exasperation, could talk only of lawn.

Carroll exploited the situation by inviting the parents and their friends the following weekend. He called it Open House, a term then gaining fashion. Everyone knew it was really Open Lawn. Despite Carroll's apparent guile, it was a self-conscious occasion for him, partly because he seriously underestimated his guests' thirsts and had to phone the pub for an emergency home delivery.

But that event changed forever local thinking about lawn and the eternal contest between house and garden. It also softened widely held views of Carroll's failings. These included, in descending order of offence, his persistent sobriety, his unflagging politeness, his three dropped catches in a single cricket match and his determined refusal to seduce the town's leading spinster. Carroll would be remembered long after that small, dishevelled town had, for him, become a hazy waypoint in his long life.

No more icebergs

A couple of the villagers claimed to have heard the collision. But they were the Naseby twins, Gerry and Clem, who sat up late most nights, drinking home brew, smoking roll-your-owns and chatting about nothing. Gerry had achieved notoriety as a teenager when his parents took him and his twin to the drive-in. Incensed by the numerical advantage enjoyed by the baddies in the film then playing, Gerry took his air rifle from the boot of the car and pinged a few of them, or at least the place on the screen they'd recently occupied. The subsequent good behaviour bond, his parents maintained until their dying days, was a blessing for everyone.

Gerry stood there now, shuffling from foot to foot, and 'reckoned' – his favourite word – he'd heard a loud whistle followed by a huge wet whack. 'Y'know the sort of sound,' he said, looking around. 'Like a soppy dishcloth hittin' someone real hard.'

Some of the women gave him a disapproving look. Our small community had its fair share of marital strains.

'Well, we can't just stand here all day, gawking,' my mother said.

Gawking was exactly what I wanted.

One of the other women asked, 'What are we going to do about it?'

'Not much we can do, is there?' said Franky Martin, shrugging his shoulders. He ran the post office and, like it, was small and badly in need of refurbishment.

'We've got to do something, haven't we?' declared Joyce Cotton, our local schoolteacher, whose prim style set her apart from most others.

'I called the police,' Franky replied. 'They might drive over later and take a look.'

'Might?' Joyce asked, irritation simmering on her voice. 'I don't think might is good enough, Franky. There needs to be an investigation. Who is going to inform the railways people? We need to know exactly what happened.'

'There's not much anyone can do now,' Franky said, shrugging again.

'There is a body and it was hit by a train and there needs to be a report. That's all I'm saying,' Joyce replied sharply.

There was an uneasy silence. Then we heard a strange sound and turned around to see Pop Ferguson pushing his wheelbarrow towards us, its metal wheel squawking on the gravelly road.

One of the kids called out, 'Takin' the barrow for a walk, Pop?'

A couple of the others sniggered.

Pop smiled. 'Thought I might as well give the dogs a good feed. Be a real shame to let all that meat go to waste.'

'No one should touch the corpse until the paperwork's completed,' Joyce declared. 'It's a sentient being and there must be a proper way of handling such an occurrence.'

'Aw, Joyce,' said Pop, shaking his head. 'You've lived here long enough to understand that most of us wouldn't even know what that bloody word means. And what we're looking at is definitely a was. So let's do something about it before there's an even bigger mess. It's January, Joyce. Need I say more?'

'Yeah, come on, Joyce,' one of the other women urged, 'there's plenty for everyone. Why don't you go and get your cart?'

Wary laughter eddied through the small gathering. Then Franky spoke again. He kept licking his lips. That made him look both nervous and with something to hide. 'Joyce, you want to do what's right. We know that. We respect you for it. But no amount of paperwork can undo what's happened.'

'Just what are you getting at, Franky?' Joyce challenged.

'Well, um, why don't we all go and get our wheelbarrows,' Franky said. 'And you, Steve,' he pointed to one of the village boys who'd just got his driving licence, 'maybe you could bring your mum's ute and we'll take the best cuts of the bull to the school and have a bit of a get together there later on. If that's okay with you, Joyce, of course,' he added quickly, alarm in his voice. 'Nowhere else to go since the hall burnt down.'

Joyce seemed to think about it for a long time. Then she said, 'Well, if you must.' Another silence followed but she added, 'Perhaps it's not such a bad idea.'

'Thank you, Joyce,' Franky said softly. He cleared his throat, took several deep breaths, then said more assuredly, 'Righto, everybody, let's get to work.'

We struggled home, our leaky barrows laden with chunks of meat and large gristly bones, wonderfully iridescent in the bright afternoon sun. The procession would be talked about for weeks afterwards. There was even a small item in *The Regional Times* headed, 'Villagers' gruesome parade'.

That night, a festive air hung over the school, encouraged in part by the overproof marinade supplied by the Naseby brothers. Most of the families arrived with potato salads and lots of home-grown tomatoes and iceberg lettuces.

The highlight of the evening, at least according to my mother, was the quiz which she and Joyce organised. The aim was not to answer questions but to come up with ones which really couldn't be answered. We broke into little groups and wrote our question on a sheet of butcher's paper. A show of hands decided the top three. The winner received six bottles of Naseby home brew and the runners-up smaller quantities. Someone suggested that the order of the prizes should be reversed. My mother chided that such a comment 'Was not in the spirit of the evening.'

Third prize went to 'Do butterflies remember being caterpillars?', second to 'Who was the first person to eat an egg?' and first to 'Do fairies perspire?' Its authors included Clem Naseby.

'Inside job,' someone exclaimed.

'All above board,' my mother declared.

By then it was getting late and a beery goodwill had embraced the crowd.

I won't pretend to have understood everything that went on that day. But there was a feeling that that our little village had shown its mettle. There'd been a killing. We'd handled it sensibly and we'd all benefited. Everyone scrubbed up for the barbecue and put on what a few of them still called their Sunday best. Maybe seeing all that mess along the railway line made them think about their own appearance. The Naseby brothers even shaved, a shock for everyone used to their coating of grey, scratchy-looking stubble.

Remarkably, or so it seemed to me, Franky and Joyce overcame their differences. During the evening, they disappeared for quite a while. I overheard a couple of the adults joking that she'd offered him a tour of the school grounds. I knew the grounds well and puzzled why it was taking them so long. When they eventually returned, I looked at them carefully. They seemed flushed, maybe a bit embarrassed. I noticed that, unusually, the top button of Joyce's blouse was undone. I wondered about that button for a long time afterwards.

A lot of years have passed since that day. They've taken with them many of the older people in the village, Pop Ferguson and Clem Naseby included. Large trucks occasionally take the short-cut through the village on the now-sealed road, the Sharapova-like squeals of their compression brakes startling the few remaining residents. Those, like me, who were once the younger generation, mostly live a long way from the village. My mother is still alive, though she struggles to recall her days there. But, starting with a chance encounter in a Sydney pub, every year in late spring a small group of us travel 'home', as we call it, getting together over a barbecue at the abandoned school building.

The food is a lot different. We don't think twice about cooking tandoori kebabs or spicy satays. The iceberg lettuces have given way to more exotic varieties, some with unpronounceable names. The tomatoes never taste as good. The food's changed. We've changed. Unfortunately, the beer hasn't. Gerry Naseby, now in his eighties and very unsteady on his legs, still turns up, driven by one of his nephews with what seems like a year's supply of home brew for the Australian military.

We joke about it and declare we won't be coming back. But we will and we all understand why. The mobile coverage is terrible, we talk to each other. And those conversations remind us of modest starts and shared journeys and how important such memories are in a world where so much just rushes by.

The hard stuff of dreams

An earlier owner had dubbed the knoll 'the lookout'. From there, it was possible to see almost all of the property. Robert first climbed the lookout soon after his arrival. It was late afternoon, with hints of autumn cool in the air. He walked quickly and it took him about twenty minutes to reach the top. Puffing slightly, a pleasant clamminess upon him, he sat down to rest on an old log, weathered to a pale grey. As his breathing steadied, a great bush stillness descended. He could still hear the twitter of tiny, unseen wrens darting in the scrub, the steady beating wings of a crow as it carved its way through the air, lonely calls echoing to its companions, the screech of cockatoos in distant trees. But they were all single, separate sounds, without the power to coalesce and overwhelm the quiet. Like the marks of oars on water, they soon disappeared without trace.

He sat there for maybe an hour. The blue gradually went out of the sky, the land was brushed first with a delicate gold, veil-like, then the calm purples and greys of the coming night. He walked down in near darkness, a great contentment within him. When he reached the house, he left off the radio and listened to the stillness.

One night, he had gone to bed early. He drifted off but later woke with a start. He lay there for some time then turned on the light. It was just before three thirty. The idea came to him quietly, unobtrusively. He got out of bed, dressed, drank a cup of tea, found the torch and climbed the lookout. The moon had set and the night was a deep, breathless black. By now, he knew the path well but how different it seemed. The torch dissected it into small, distinct spasms of light, each tree and clump of sinewy grass and lichen-touched rock displaying an individuality of form and colour he had not absorbed before.

When he reached the top, he swung the torch slowly in a circle, taking in the detail of what previously had only been whole, tree trunks and branches and sprays of leaves nuzzling into each other and the little contours and deformities of the ground. As he moved, the shadows from the old grey log licked at his feet.

Besides its lone street lamp, a couple of lights still showed faintly in the village. He wondered if anyone there would see him and puzzle over the strange ritual he might be performing. He sat down on the log and switched off the torch. The world became seamless. It was cold and he turned up the collar of the old, stained overcoat he wore. The steady beat of a mopoke further along the ridge sounded against the pulse and scurries of the bush. A couple of the village dogs called out in useless, broken barks. One of his dogs answered and he was tempted to shout it down. He held off and it went quiet anyway. Robert became part of the night.

The faintest hint of a clear dawn showed as he walked down the pathway to the house. He sluiced his chilled hands and face with warm water, and drank cup after cup of strong, sugary tea. Then he went outside, freed the dogs and watched the sun rise effortlessly over the distant hills. Helen and the children would soon join him. Used to the different pace and demands of the city, it would be a bit of a shock for them. But he would make them happy here. He would not fail them.

A feeling of elation stayed with him for the rest of the day.

*

Just after two fifteen, a thick swirl of dust appeared on the road. Greg's car, a late-model Holden, eventually emerged.

Standing on the back veranda, Robert waited until it pulled up then called out, 'G'day, come on in.'

'G'day,' Greg returned. He was carrying a buff-coloured folder. 'By the way, Robert, this is Andrew Smythe, just arrived for a stint here. Thought I'd show him how we can work things out in tough times.'

'G'day, Andrew. Cme on in for yer lesson,' Robert grinned, adding 'How's the drought round your way?'

'Same as here I'm afraid, Mr Fortune, a crippler.'

'Yeah, bloody crippled us all right.'

Helen greeted them as they entered the living room. 'Tea or coffee?' she asked.

'Tea please,' Greg replied.

'Yeah, tea'd be fine, thanks,' Andrew said.

Helen made the tea, quickly, and brought it in. Greg was perspiring, the house creaked, a crow cawed nearby.

Greg said with a forced smile. 'Well, don't suppose we should beat around the bush. What have you got for me?'

'Depends what you got for us,' Robert replied.

Greg looked at him oddly. 'Well, in the folder,' he pointed to the table, 'there's a notice to quit. Told you I had to draw it up. Now that you have a cheque for me, don't think we're going to have to use it. I'm glad.'

'Guess we'll all be pretty glad soon,' Robert said flatly. He took a long drink of tea. His hands trembled as he put the cup back on the saucer.

There was silence except for the crow and the steady beat of cicadas.

'Guess we'd better get this over with then,' Greg prompted again, uneasily.

'Yeah, guess we better,' Robert echoed. He stood up suddenly and said, 'Aw, shit, that bloody crow's drivin' me nuts.' He disappeared quickly through the screen door onto the back veranda.

They heard a single shot, the crow again, a pause, then two more shots in rapid succession, much closer but curiously muffled.

There was a thunk as if a heavy object had been placed carefully on the floor. Robert reappeared through the kitchen, rifle in his right hand, a length of thin white rope in the left. They looked at him carefully, puzzlement on Helen's face, alarm on Greg's and Andrew's.

'Robert,' Helen said, uncertainly.

He came close to her. She could smell whisky on his breath. He leaned and said softly, his voice trembling, 'I'm so, so sorry, love.' As he did so, he swung the rifle up to her chest, very quickly, and fired. The sound reverberated around the room. Helen was driven backwards into the chair, a look of immense anguish and shock on her face. She tried to speak but a pink froth smothered her words. Minutes seemed to pass, Helen gasping, then she slumped gently in the chair.

Greg yelled, a thin, screeching, frightened sound, 'Robert, for God's sake!'

Robert took a couple of agile steps towards him and screamed 'Shuddup, Greggie, shuddup. I'll drill ya right there, ya bastard. Shuddup and lie on the floor, you fat slug! Last warning, Mr Banker!'

Greg dropped uncertainly to his hands and knees.

Andrew sat wide-eyed, ashen-faced. A shudder passed through him.

Robert scooped up the rope from the floor with the barrel of the rifle and threw it to him. 'Tie that bastard up,' he demanded, 'and do a decent fuckin' job.'

Andrew tied Greg's hands behind his back, then looped the rope down to his ankles, pinned them together and tied it off tightly.

Robert checked the knots and, satisfied, stood up. 'Now where's that bit of paper?'

'Wwwhat bbit a pppaper, Mmr Ffortune?'

'Bit a paper tellin me ta get off me fuckin' property, son. What bit a paper ya fuckin' well think I'm talkin' about?'

'I told you where it was, I told you,' Greg moaned.

'Did I ask you, big mouth? Did I?' Robert yelled. 'Well, get it fer me son,' he screamed at Andrew, 'get it fer me. What are ya, deaf or somethin'?'

Andrew moved to the table. The folder trembled violently with the shake of his hand.

'C'mon, c'mon, ya useless bastard,' Robert demanded. Then his voice softened, to mockery. 'Oh, bit of a tremble in the old paws, son. Glad I won't have ta wash your bloody underpants tonight.'

Greg whimpered. 'Please, Robert, please.'

'Aw what's up, Greggie? Things not runnin' the bank's way fer once?

Jeez, that's tough, mate.' He took the paper from Andrew. 'Sit down, son, while I read this!'

Robert sat on the right arm of Helen's chair. The front of her dress was steeped red. He caressed her bloodied cheek, looked at Andrew and said, 'Take this, son, and fold it up real small. C'mon, get goin'!'

The folding was greatly hampered by the shake in Andrew's hands. 'No hurry, son, no hurry, everythin' under control now,' Robert reassured. 'Got all day, son. Relax and take ya time.'

Greg had recovered enough to croak 'You're mad, Robert, mad. Stop this, please.' His face glistened.

'Aw, Greggie, ya poor old thing, bit bloody stressful, is it? Bit 'ard on me too, mate, I can tell you that. Specially with the kids.'

A terrible, low groan escaped from Greg. It spun desperately around the room then fled through the windows.

'Yeah,' Robert continued, his voice now very soft, 'can see that's upset ya. Was pretty upsettin' to have to do it.' He spat on the floor near Greg. 'To be quite honest, probably the most upsettin' thing I've ever had to do.'

He spat again and his voice strengthened. 'But I did it 'cause I didn't have a choice. You're the bank, mate, so your word goes. Well, I think you've said enough. Best if ya keep ya trap shut from now on. In fact, yer little mate's got somethin' ta keep you quiet, somethin' to chew on.' Robert snapped at Andrew, 'Put that fuckin' bit a paper in his mouth, son. Eat it, you bastard!' he shouted at Greg. 'Eat it or I'll blow your fuckin' balls off.'

Andrew bent over Greg, who half-opened his mouth. Andrew pushed the paper in. Greg gagged then seemed to clear his throat and began to chew the paper slowly.

Suddenly Robert stood up, advanced towards Greg, pressed the rifle barrel into his ear and said in a low voice, 'By the way, Greggie, by the way, keep chewin', mate.' Then he chanted, 'Chew Greggie, chew Greggie, chew Greggie, chew!'

He swung the rifle on Andrew and said, 'How long d'ya say y've been with the bank, son?'

'Bbbit over a yyyear,' Andrew stammered.

'Aw, well y're really only a lackey then, aren't ya? Pity yer payin' such a high price for deliverin' a bit a paper. Now get down on the bloody floor. Face down. Now!'

Andrew sunk to the floor, deathly white. Robert came up close, held the rifle to the back of Andrew's head and fired.

'Jeez, Greggie, that was a bit nasty, wasn't it? Bit like a fuckin' execution. Anyway, that's the way it goes, I reckon. Guess that just leaves you'n me now, doesn't it? How we goin' to sort this one out, mate? C'mon, give us one of your bright ideas!'

Greg tried to say something but could only mouth soundless words. Papery saliva drooled from the corners of his mouth.

'Look, mate, don't want you to think I'm bein' rude or anythin' like that but I've got a phone call to make. Just one. I'll be over there,' he stabbed the rifle towards the corner, 'so you won't get lonely or anythin' like that. In fact, I'll tell you what, Greggie, you can listen in if you like, I won't be put out by you eavesdroppin', not a bit.'

Robert walked to the telephone and dialled. He took a deep, shuddering breath. There was tightness and tremor in his voice. 'Aw g'day. (Pause). Do I? No, everythin's fine mate, fine. Weather a bit too bloody fine as usual. (Pause). Wonder if you'd mind doin' something for me. I can't go into details but it'll all be clear pretty soon. (Pause) No, just hear me out will you. Could you give the cops a call in about ten minutes or so? Ask them to get out here soon as they can. (Pause). Well, I just can't. (Pause) No, don't come yourself. Please don't. (Pause) I've got to go, mate, thanks for everythin'. You've been the best neighbours anyone could wish for.'

He put the phone down. There was an urgency in his voice now. 'We'd better keep goin', Greggie, before the crowd comes. I'll just get things ready.' He disappeared into the kitchen briefly and was then standing in the doorway, jerry can in hand. 'Oh, Greggie, you're a clever one, you are. Can tell by the look in your eyes you've got it all worked out.'

'You're mad, you're mad, you're mad,' Greg whimpered.

'That all ya can say? That all!? Not too bloody original. But ya might just be right. Might be completely out of my tree, mate. And you and your fuckin' bank had a bit to do with it. Had a whole lot in fact.'

The tension drained from his voice and he said calmly, 'Anyway, just got to get on with it, haven't we, keep pluggin' away.'

Robert went into the kitchen again, returned with a half empty bottle of Johnny Walker, pulled the cork and took a long swig. 'Want one, mate?' he asked sarcastically. 'No, s'pose it'd be better if you didn't. Take away the taste of the paper. Wouldn't want to do that, would we now?'

He laid the rifle down on the table, opened the jerry can and splashed a vaporous circle around Greg. He turned, spat on the floor again, doused Helen and then Andrew. The air reeked.

'Yeah,' he said flatly, 's'pose I'd better give the kids a splash too.' He disappeared for a few moments, returned and emptied the jerrycan haphazardly around the room. Then calmly he retrieved the whisky bottle and the rifle, dragged a chair next to Helen, leaned over and kissed her bloodied lips, sat down and stroked her cheek.

Greg watched soundlessly, terror and defeat in his eyes. Robert placed the rifle between his knees, took another long swig, threw the bottle heavily onto the floor and extracted a box of matches from the breast pocket of his shirt.

There was a sudden gush of flame, a single shot, and Greg's long, long scream.

Acknowledgements

'The spider's web of memory': an earlier version of this story, 'Mrs Browning's legacy', was shortlisted in the 2018 Fish Publishing short story competition.

'Our fern garden': first published in *Betrayals*, Ginninderra Press, 2002

'The right call?': published in the Newcastle Writers Centre short story award shortlist, 2018.

'My island home': runner-up in the 2016 E.J. Brady Short Story Competition.

'God's honest truth': an earlier version of this story, 'A Balibo Christmas Tale', was first published in *Quadrant*, January–February 2001.

'The greatest game': first published by *Eureka Street* magazine, 2006.

'A tongue lashing': shortlisted in the Fish Publishing 2018 flash fiction competition.

'Your call cannot be connected': an earlier version of this story was longlisted in the Fish Publishing 2019 flash fiction competition.

'Dr Watson wrestles with his work-life balance' was developed from the author's novel *Beethoven's Tenth and the journey which saved the world*, 2020.

'Bathurst for beginners': an earlier version of this story was broadcast on ABC Radio and included in the ABC CD *Short Stories from 'round Australia*, 2004.

'Going bush': an earlier version of this story was first published in *The Canberra Times*, December 2000.

'House and garden': an earlier version of this story was published by *The Canberra Times*, December 2000.

'The hard stuff of dreams': an earlier version of this story, 'Bank Closed Until Further Notice,' won the 2001 Outback Writers' Centre Centenary of Federation short story competition.